Vivien collided with brilliant eyes as dark as jet.

When the darkness of his intent gaze suddenly flamed gold, her heart lurched as though Lucca had aimed a kick at it. Her breath was trapped in her dry throat, her heartbeat pounding behind her ribs. She felt as if she was standing on the edge of a precipice, only the fear that gripped her was also laced with helpless longing. The desire she had made herself forget during their separation had flared up again inside her, as though someone had tossed a flaming torch on a bale of hay.

Her voice emerged husky and breathless as she forced herself to concentrate long enough to say what she knew she needed to say.

"I still have feelings for you and I'm asking you to give our marriage another chance. I want you back."

Intense satisfaction of the darkest kind engulfed Lucca. "You want me back?"

Vivien jerked her chin in affirmation. "Yes, I want you back," she re_____ The buzz of fierce s_____ had thickened the a_____

"It's not mutual," Luc___

Dear Reader,

The Mistress Wife is my fiftieth book, and a celebration of all my favorite elements of romance. Lucca and Vivien rediscover their love in the gorgeous Tuscan countryside, but, as always, it requires give-and-take on both sides.

Mediterranean men and strong and sassy heroines power my stories. I like emotional characters, fast-moving plots and romances which seethe with all the passion, heartbreak and love we all experience in the world.

I would like to thank all at Harlequin Presents® and all my readers for the wonderful support that has been my inspiration since I began writing.

Best wishes,

Lynne Graham

Lynne Graham

THE MISTRESS WIFE

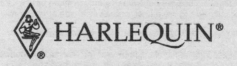

TORONTO • NEW YORK • LONDON
AMSTERDAM • PARIS • SYDNEY • HAMBURG
STOCKHOLM • ATHENS • TOKYO • MILAN • MADRID
PRAGUE • WARSAW • BUDAPEST • AUCKLAND

ISBN 0-373-12428-7

THE MISTRESS WIFE

First North American Publication 2004.

Copyright © 2004 by Lynne Graham.

www.eHarlequin.com

Printed in U.S.A.

CHAPTER ONE

'I WASN'T sure whether or not you would want to see this...' Speaking in the uneasy tone of one apologising in advance for a potential offence, Lucca's cousin, Alfredo, settled a tabloid newspaper down on the elegant glass desk.

At first glimpse of the smirking blonde displaying her bountiful curves in the centre of a page topped by garish headlines, Lucca Saracino froze, his lean, powerful face hardening. It was Jasmine Bailey, the bimbo whose lies had contributed to the destruction of his marriage. Now yesterday's news as far as the rich and famous were concerned, Jasmine was plumbing even sleazier depths with the no-holds-barred revelations of exactly how low she had had to sink to achieve her original fifteen minutes of fame. In that uninhibited telling, the former topless model freely confessed that she had concocted her story about having shared a wild night of passion with the Italian billionaire, Lucca Saracino, on his luxury yacht.

'You should sue her!' Alfredo, a stockily built young man in his early twenties, urged with all the eager but unsophisticated zeal of a recent law graduate keen to prove his mettle.

Such an exercise would be futile, Lucca reflected, wide, sensual mouth assuming a sardonic curl. He would gain nothing from dragging a cheap little scrubber and his own long-lost reputation through the courts. More to the point, his divorce was about to be made final. Vivien, his soon-to-be ex-wife, had judged him guilty with a speed and lack of trust that would have shocked any male with a sense of fair play. Lifting her virginal little head high, Vivien had donned the mantle of saintly, suffering piety and vacated the marital home. Encouraged by her sour and money-hungry sister, Bernice, Vivien had walked out on their marriage in spite of the fact that she'd been carrying their first child. She had refused to listen to his declaration of innocence. The woman who wept buckets over Lassie films had shown him a face of stone.

'Lucca...?' Alfredo prompted in the brooding silence that every other member of Lucca's personal staff would have read as a tacit warning.

With difficulty, Lucca suppressed an exasperated rebuke. Allowing his gormless cousin to work for him even temporarily had been an act of charity on his part. Alfredo was desperate to add some business experience to his unimpressive CV. Lucca had found him clever but impractical, conscientious but uninspired, well meaning but tactless. While others soared, Alfredo would always plod and often infuriate.

'I owe you a big apology,' the younger man continued awkwardly, standing square in front of the desk and evidently determined to say his piece. 'I didn't believe the Bailey woman had set you up. My parents didn't either. We all thought you *had* been playing away!'

Every low suspicion of the level of that side of the family's faith in him now fully confirmed, Lucca veiled grim dark golden eyes.

'And absolutely nobody blamed you in the slightest,' Alfredo hastened to assert. 'Vivien just didn't fit the bill—'

'Vivien is the mother of my son. Don't speak of her with anything other than the respect that is her due,' Lucca murmured in icy reproof.

Alfredo flushed and hurried to offer profuse apologies instead. Impatient with his essential stupidity, Lucca dismissed him from his presence. Rising from his seat, he strode over to the imposing windows that proffered a spectacular view of London, but his forbidding gaze was turned inward and his thoughts were relentlessly bitter.

His infant son, Marco, was growing up without him in a mean little home where Italian was not spoken. There had been nothing civilised about the breakup of his marriage or the separation that had followed. Lucca had had to fight hard for what little he saw of the child he adored. He had been branded an unfaithful husband by Jasmine Bailey's sleazy allegations. His lawyers had made it plain to him that he had no hope whatsoever of winning guardianship of his son from an estranged wife with an irreproachable reputation. It utterly outraged Lucca's sense of justice that Vivien, who had wrecked their marriage with her distrust, should have effortlessly retained custody of his child.

He knew himself to be at best an occasional visitor on the outskirts of Marco's life and he was afraid that his son forgot him altogether between visits. How could so young a child remember an absentee father between one month and the next? There was no way either that Vivien would be reminding Marco of the parent she had deprived him of possessing. But now there was also no way that she would be able to retain occupancy of the moral high ground...

As that tantalising reality pierced Lucca's brooding reflections it was like a shot of adrenalin slivering through his lean, powerful frame with life-giving force. His luxuriant lashes lowered on eyes that suddenly glowed tiger-bright with scorching satisfaction. He pondered the very real possibility that Vivien might miss out on seeing Jasmine Bailey's confession. An academic who took little interest in the everyday world, Vivien rarely read newspapers.

Lucca buzzed his secretary, instructed her to obtain a pristine new copy of the relevant paper and have it delivered to Vivien with a gift card bearing his compliments. Petty? He didn't think so. Pride demanded that he draw her attention to the proof of his innocence.

It would spoil Vivien's day and worse. Vivien had led a sheltered life. Naïve as she was, she bruised easily. She had the sort of conscience that kept her awake at night and would suffer the tortures of the damned when she was forced to face the truth that she had misjudged her husband. Natural justice might finally be operating on his behalf but nothing could make the punishment fit the crime, could it?

'Please come out, Jock…' Vivien begged the three-legged Scottie dog hiding under the sideboard.

Jock, rather optimistically named after a genial cartoon character, stayed put. He had been denied the chance to get his teeth into the leg of the washing-machine repairman and therefore cruelly prevented from fulfilling his duty to protect his mistress from a male interloper. Dogs were not supposed to sulk but Jock went off in a huff if he was denied the delights of chasing male individuals from the premises.

Marco gave a gurgle of delight and began crawling under the sideboard to join his favourite playmate.

Vivien scooped her son up. Huge brown eyes fringed by silky black lashes as long as fly swats reproached her for her interference. Marco made a determined squirming motion in an effort to escape his mother's restraining arms and when that failed loosed a noisy shout of annoyance.

Vivien steeled herself for a battle. 'No...' she told Marco quietly and steadily, all too painfully aware after a recent very public humiliation at the supermarket that it was time that she learned how to handle her son's fits of temper.

No? In visible disbelief, Marco gazed back at the fair-haired woman with her big anxious green eyes. No? His nanny, Rosa, used that unpleasant word to him, and his father too. But he knew his mother adored him, and loved to please him. Indeed at the age of eighteen months he had all the controlling instincts of a tyrant, who had already discovered that he needed only the most basic of weapons to triumph over all opposition: when thwarted, he threw unmanageable tantrums until he got what he wanted. He began to draw in a deep, deep breath in preparation for screaming and raging his way to a crushing victory.

Barely five feet two inches tall and of slender build, Vivien laid her solid little son down inside the playpen. Marco was strong and when he flailed around in a temper, she found it very difficult to hold him. Once he had fallen off her lap and bumped his head. After that scare she had begun putting him down for his own safety.

'He's a spoilt brat!' her sister, Bernice, had condemned with a shudder of distaste that had cut Vivien's tender maternal heart to the quick.

'Demanding little chap, isn't he?' Fabian Garsdale,

her friend and colleague in the botany department, had remarked with an air of shocked disapproval when he'd witnessed such a display. 'Have you thought of applying a spot of good old-fashioned discipline?'

'You must try really hard to be firm with him,' Rosa, Marco's part-time nanny, had advised when pressed to explain why her charge rarely subjected her to the same temperamental episodes. 'Marco can be very strong-willed.'

Vivien performed a handstand beside the playpen. If she was quick off the mark, simply distracting Marco worked a treat. Mid-wail, her son paused for breath and then chortled with delighted surprise at the sight of his mother upside down. He sat up to get a better view and his glorious smile shone forth.

Flipping back upright again, Vivien swept him into her arms, hugged him tight and blinked back the moisture in her eyes. All the fierce agonising love that she had once felt for Lucca had been transferred to their son. Without Marco, she was convinced that she would have gone out of her mind with grief over her broken marriage. It had been her baby's needs that first forced her to confront unpleasant realities and carve out a new life for them both. But the devastating pain of Lucca's betrayal was still locked up inside her and she had to live with it daily. She had always felt things too deeply and had learnt as a child to conceal the embarrassing intensity of her feelings behind a quiet façade. To do otherwise made people uncomfortable.

The noise of a car pulling rather too fast into the gravel driveway outside announced Bernice's return. Jock emerged from below the sideboard, uttered a single bark, looked nervously at the sitting-room door and then went into retreat again. A moment later, the door bounced back in protest on its hinges to frame a tall, leggy brunette, who would have been quite stunningly lovely had it not been for the angry hardness of her blue eyes and the clenched set of dissatisfaction marring her mouth.

Indifferent to Bernice's, entrance for his aunt never gave him attention unless it was to lament his vocal output or his infuriatingly immature behaviour, Marco gave vent to a large sleepy yawn and rested back heavily in his mother's arms.

Bernice sent the curly-headed toddler a look of irritation. 'Shouldn't the kid be having his nap?'

'I was just about to take him up.' Wondering sympathetically if her sister had suffered yet another disappointment in the employment stakes, Vivien went upstairs and tried not to worry about her own increasingly strained finances.

After all, it would be downright cruel to preach economy yet again to Bernice, who was already utterly miserable struggling to survive without champagne breakfasts and the like. Vivien was also guiltily conscious that her own personal reluctance to take anything other than the barest minimum financial assistance from Lucca after their separation was ultimately responsible for her overdraft at the bank. She had put pride ahead of common sense and was now paying the literal price.

At least, the cottage was small and, now that all the repairs had been done, economical to run. Of course, Bernice said it was only fit for dolls. But in the dark days of late pregnancy when Vivien had been alone and struggling to bear a life that did not contain even occasional glimpses of Lucca, the little house had seemed like a sanctuary. Embellished by a mature tree in the front garden, the cottage lay in pretty countryside not too far from the Oxford college where Vivien currently worked three days a week as a tutor in the botany department.

Vivien squeezed between her own bed and Marco's cot and tucked her son in for his morning nap. Possessed of two narrow bedrooms, her diminutive home was the perfect size for a single parent of one but stretched to capacity when required to house another adult. Even so, Vivien was overjoyed to have her sibling's company and only wished she had foreseen the possibility that she might one day require roomier accommodation. Yet who could have guessed that her sister's designer boutique in London would fail? Her poor sister had lost everything: her trendy Docklands apartment, her smart sports car, not to mention the majority of her fashionable but fickle friends.

'Don't even bother asking me how my interview went!' her sister hissed furiously when Vivien joined her again. 'The cheeky old hag virtually accused me of lying on my CV and I told her what she could do with her lousy hotel job!'

Vivien was taken aback 'Surely the woman didn't accuse you of lying—'

'She didn't *have* to…she started asking me questions in French and I hadn't a clue what she was rattling on about!' Bernice proclaimed in outrage. 'I claimed a working knowledge of French on my CV…I didn't say I was practically bilingual!'

Although it was news to Vivien that the sibling three years her senior had even a working knowledge of the French language, she hurried to soothe ruffled feathers with words of sympathy.

Unimpressed, Bernice pursed her lips. 'It's *your* fault that I was humiliated!'

'My fault?' Vivien stilled in dismay.

'You're still married to an incredibly rich man and yet we're practically starving!' Bernice condemned with ferocious bitterness. 'You're always moaning about how broke you are and making me feel guilty...I'm chasing rotten jobs way below my capabilities and you're sitting home on your bum most of the week spoiling Marco like he's a royal prince!'

Vivien was appalled at the level of her sister's resentment and felt horribly responsible for her own deficiencies. 'Bernice, I—'

'You always were weird, Vivien. Look at your life!' her angry sister urged with contemptuous clarity. 'You live out here in the back of beyond with your freaky dog and precious son and you never do anything or go any place worth mentioning. You work in a boring job, live a boring life and have always been the most boring person I know. I wasn't surprised when Lucca took to adultery on the ocean waves with a sexy blonde! The wonder was that he *ever* married a nonentity like you!'

Beneath that tirade, Vivien had turned white as milk. Bernice slammed into the sitting room and the cottage shook with the force of the door shuddering shut. Resolutely, Vivien thrust Bernice's hurtful words down into her subconscious. Fondling Jock's ears to soothe his trembling, for loud voices upset him, Vivien reminded herself that her sister was going through a very unhappy time, which would have challenged anyone's temper to the utmost. Nobody knew better than Vivien that it was tough building a new life out of the ashes of loss and destruction. It was particularly dif-

ficult for Bernice, who had never had to make compromises and who had taken her once privileged world
entirely for granted.

In comparison, Vivien had been brought up to believe that she was an incredibly lucky little girl. Her
birth mother and father might have died in a car accident when she was only months old but she had been
swiftly placed for adoption with the affluent and so-
cially prominent Dillon family. Their daughter,
Bernice, had been just three years old and the couple
had been eager to adopt a little girl to ensure that
Bernice would never want for company.

Nobody had ever been unkind to Vivien in the
Dillon household but she had failed to fulfil her adoptive parents' fond hope that she would become
Bernice's best friend. Bernice and Vivien had had
nothing in common and the age gap between the two
girls had only underlined the differences. Sensitive to
a fault, Vivien had grown up with the guilt-making
awareness that she seemed to be a source of continual
disappointment to her family. The Dillons had hoped
that Vivien would be a girlie girl like Bernice, who
would delight in fashion, ponies and ballet before
branching out into fashion, young men and a wild social whirl.

Instead, Vivien had been shy and retiring and the
clumsiest little girl in the ballet class. Horses had
scared her only a little less than young men and she
had avoided parties like the plague. A bookworm from
the instant she'd learned to read, she had been confident only in the academic world where her intelligence
was rewarded with top exam grades awarded at an
early age. Her achievements in that line however had
merely embarrassed her parents, who felt that it was

somehow not quite normal for a young woman to be quite so keen on studying.

Her mother had died of a heart attack when Vivien was seventeen. She had been at university when her father had passed away after many months of stress following severe financial reverses. Bernice had been hit very hard by the sale of the Dillon family home and the beautiful antiques, which she had grown up believing would one day be hers. Vivien had found it impossible to comfort her sibling for that loss.

The shrill of the doorbell startled Vivien out of an anxious re-examination of her failings as an adoptive daughter and sister. A courier passed her a package and raced away again on his motorbike.

'What is it?' Bernice demanded from behind Vivien as the smaller woman stared down dumbfounded at the elegant gilded card bearing her estranged husband's signature in a careless black scrawl.

'I don't know.' Having assumed the parcel contained a present for Marco, Vivien frowned in confusion when she found a newspaper inside the quite ludicrously opulent gift bag.

Instantly, she froze, for she recognised the photo of the voluptuous blonde promising to spill all her secrets on page five. Her tummy quivered and flipped with nausea and her palms grew damp. Why on earth would Lucca be so fantastically cruel as to send her an article about Jasmine Bailey? She thumbed clumsily to the relevant page, deaf to her sister's piercing demand that she pass the publication to her.

Finding the headline of LIES MADE MY FORTUNE, Vivien read the first few paragraphs of the double-page spread three times over. With a total lack of even rudimentary shame, Jasmine confessed in print that her claim to have slept with Lucca Saracino had been an elaborate and highly effective lie couched to gain her publicity and win her invites to society parties. The wild all-night bout of adulterous passion, which the glamour model had described in such disgusting detail just two short years earlier, had been a complete fabrication.

Vivien was welded to the spot by a curious spreading numbness that appeared to be threatening her brain as much as her body. Perspiration dampened her brow. Jasmine Bailey had made up her story? It *had* all been a wicked lie? Her stomach felt hollow. Lucca had not betrayed his marital vows. Lucca had been true to her...and she? *And she?* She had believed the very worst of him and discounted his denials. She had turned her back on her husband and their marriage. That rolling agony of horrifying truth swallowed Vivien alive. It was like falling into an abyss and drowning.

'I got it all wrong...I misjudged Lucca...'

'You...you did what?' her sister questioned loudly, impatience impelling her to snatch the newspaper from Vivien's loosened grasp.

Vivien raised a trembling hand to her brow where unbearable tension was pounding out a drumbeat of self-blame. Her mind just could not cope with the enormity of Jasmine Bailey's confession. It had hit her like a brick on glass and shattered her. The world she had remade had been shattered with it. In the space of a moment she had gone from being a woman who believed she had been right to walk away from her unfaithful husband to a woman who had made a huge and appalling mistake that had damaged both the man she loved and their child.

'Surely you're not being taken in by this rubbish?' Bernice queried on a cutting note of scornful dismissal. 'Now that she's yesterday's news, Jasmine Bailey would say or do anything to get her name back into the headlines!'

'But not that…her story tallies with exactly what Lucca said at the time, only…' Vivien's voice lost power and then regrouped in a choky tone as her throat convulsed on the tears she was fighting back. 'Only I wouldn't *listen* to him—'

'Of course you didn't listen!' her sister snapped. 'You had too much sense to listen to his lies. You knew he was a notorious womaniser even before you married him. Didn't I try to warn you?'

A lot of people had tried to warn Vivien off marrying Lucca Saracino. Nobody had been happy about their union. Not his family and friends and not her own either. Everyone had been astonished and then critical of the chances of such an apparent mismatch lasting. Supposed well-wishers had variously told Vivien that she was too quiet, too reserved, too old-fashioned, too academic and insufficiently exciting for a male of Lucca's smooth sophistication. She had dutifully listened to all the concerned onlookers and her confidence had been battered low even before the wedding. At the end of the day, however, Lucca would still only have had to snap his fingers for her to have come running across a field of flames. She had loved him more than life itself and had been as lost and helpless as a child against the power of that love.

'You're virtually divorced now anyway,' Bernice reminded the smaller, slighter woman sharply. 'You should never have married him. You were totally unsuited.'

Vivien said nothing. She was staring into space, momentarily lost in her own feverish thoughts. Lucca had not, after all, betrayed her in Jasmine Bailey's arms. The tacky blonde had pretty much conned her way onto Lucca's yacht in the first place, Vivien recalled dully. Passing herself off as a student, Jasmine had been hired by one of Lucca's guests to act as a companion to his adolescent daughter during the cruise and help her improve her English. When Jasmine had gone public with her colourful tale of a night of stolen passion nobody had been in a position to confirm or contradict her claims. Nobody but Lucca...

Vivien felt sick. She had punished her husband for a sin he had not committed. Instead of having faith in the man she had married, she had abandoned faith. Lucca had been innocent, which meant that all the agonising unhappiness she had endured since then was entirely of her own making. That was a very tough reality for Vivien to accept but she had sufficient humility to soon achieve it and move on to the far more important point of facing the great wrong that she had inflicted on Lucca. Her mind was as clear as a bell on what she ought to do next.

'I need to see Lucca...' Vivien breathed.

'Haven't you listened to *anything* I've said?' Bernice demanded. 'What on earth would you need to see Lucca for?'

Vivien was in the grip of shock and acting on automatic pilot but, regardless, the overpowering necessity of seeing Lucca in the flesh shone like a beacon in the darkness of her turmoil. It was almost two years since she had last laid eyes on him. Lawyers had dealt with the legal proceedings and a nanny collected Marco for his visits with his father. Lucca's immense wealth had ensured that there was no requirement for him to tolerate a more personal connection with his estranged wife.

'I have to see him.' Vivien was slowly, clumsily striving to consider the practicalities of travelling up to London. As it was a day on which Vivien usually worked, Rosa would soon be arriving to look after Marco and would stay until six that evening. 'Are you going out tonight?'

Surprised by that change of subject, Bernice frowned. 'I've nothing organised…'

'Goodness knows what time I'll get to see Lucca. I expect I'll be very low on his list of welcome visitors. So I'll probably be back late,' Vivien explained anxiously. 'I can arrange for Rosa to stay longer and put Marco to bed. Could you babysit until I get home?'

'If you go anywhere near Lucca, you'll be making the biggest mistake of your life!' Bernice swore in vehement annoyance.

'I have to tell him how sorry I am…that's the very least of what I owe him,' Vivien pointed out tightly.

In the strained silence that fell, a calculating light entered Bernice's appraisal. 'Possibly it's not such a bad idea after all. You could use the opportunity to tell Lucca that you are hopelessly broke—'

Vivien flinched. 'I *couldn't!*'

'Then I won't be able to look after Marco,' her sister countered without hesitation.

Frustration and embarrassment fought inside Vivien. 'All right…I'll raise the subject and see if something can be sorted out…'

Her capitulation made Bernice smile with amused triumph. 'Fine…then just this once I'll babysit. Let's hope that when Lucca sees you grovelling, he feels excessively generous.'

Informed of Vivien's arrival, Lucca rose and called a five-minute break in the meeting he was chairing.

Able to view his estranged wife through the glass partition that surrounded the reception area, Lucca stilled on the landing above. In the vast, opulent space below, Vivien looked small, slight and insignificant. Her brown top and skirt were shapeless and ill fitting and she probably owned at least three sets of the same outfit. She hated shopping and buying in triplicate helped her to avoid it. Shorn of his care and attention, she had regressed from the standards he set at shocking speed and barricaded herself back into her unfashionable shell. Her nails were unpainted, her silky blonde hair caught up rather messily in a cheap plastic clip.

In her current guise, she was not a woman likely to turn male heads at first glance. Yet she possessed a luminous beauty that not even the dullest presentation could conceal. His keen gaze lingered on the visible slice of narrow shoulder blessed with skin as opalescent as a pearl and moved on to the delicate perfection of her profile and the tantalising femininity of her slim, restive hands and slender ankles. A raw flame of desire blistered through his big, powerful frame and rage at his own lack of control surged in its wake and balled his own hands into hard fists.

Once, he recalled bleakly, he had thought her sweet and unspoilt and loyal unto death. Her warmth and modesty had enchanted him and her honesty and kindness had made a huge impression on his cynical view of the world. There had been nothing false about her.

He had truly believed he had struck gold. He had believed that his marriage would work where so many others broke down. He was a man to whom failure of any kind was anathema and he had chosen his wife with great care and caution. Yet she had proved completely unworthy of the ring he had put on her finger.

Righteous derision made him look away from her and the chill of intellectual control soon cooled the fire in his blood. For what good reason had he walked straight out on an important meeting? His essential courtesy had momentarily misled him, he decided, swinging on his heel to return to the conference table. After all, he had not invited Vivien to storm his office in the middle of his working day and demand his attention.

Her response to Jasmine Bailey's confession in print was, however, very typical of her and he could have predicted it, Lucca conceded grimly. He knew Vivien well. Indeed, he had once prided himself on the reality that he excelled at everything at which she was useless. For all her apparent outward calm, Vivien could react with staggering impulsiveness and wildly undisciplined emotion. She was always uniformly blind to the darker motivations of others. She was a leading authority on rare ferns but she could neither recognise nor protect herself from the arts of calculation and manipulation. She would struggle to find a redeeming quality in even the most dislikeable human being.

But Lucca had no desire to be redeemed in her eyes. He did not wish to see her either and regarded her spontaneous arrival at his office as a piece of foolishness, likely to plunge her into embarrassment. To stage her descent on the same day that Jasmine Bailey confessed her lies to the world was exceptionally bad timing. Had Vivien no sense whatsoever? He had often thought not. If the press realised where she was, the paparazzi would arrive in hordes. Angling his wide shoulders back beneath his superbly tailored grey suit jacket, Lucca strode back to his meeting.

Unaware that she had been under observation, Vivien took a seat. She was flustered and uneasy at the covert stares she was attracting. On the train, she had tried to contact Lucca by phone and failed. Once she had had a private number for his mobile phone but that number was no longer operational. He had been 'unavailable' when she'd phoned the Saracino building. When she had asked for the means to contact him in person, she had been coolly told that only Lucca could give out that information. Dismayed by the confidential wall holding her at bay, she had rung off again without requesting an appointment. Told on arrival that Lucca was exceptionally busy, she prepared herself for a long wait and comforted herself with the reflection that at least Lucca was in the building and not abroad on business as he might well have been.

At five that evening Lucca closed his meeting and instructed a member of his staff to show Vivien into his office. Having waited for almost three hours without a word of encouragement and with steadily shrinking expectations, Vivien was hugely relieved to be escorted out of the reception area. But she was a jelly of nerves at the very thought of seeing Lucca again after so long. She did not know what she was going to say to him. She had no idea how to bridge the enormous chasm between them. His supposed infidelity had formed a giant barrier between her and her emotions and now that barrier was gone and with it the script of how she was to behave.

Flustered and unsure of herself, Vivien walked through the door.

Lucca stood centre stage in his cool, contemporary office, effortlessly dominating his surroundings. Six feet three inches tall and gifted with the superb build of a natural athlete, he was an exceptionally good-looking guy with an overwhelmingly physical impact. All the oxygen Vivien needed to breathe seemed to vanish from the atmosphere. Her mouth ran dry and her heart thumped. Colliding with his stunning dark eyes was like falling on an electric fence. She was embarrassed and rather ashamed that at such a crucial moment she could still be so immediately aware of his magnetic attraction

'So...' murmured Luca, whose machinations in business had once led to him being described as smooth as black ice and twice as treacherous. His gorgeous accent sizzled along the single drawn-out word and sent a reflexive shiver down her taut backbone. 'What brings you up from the country?'

CHAPTER TWO

DISCONCERTED entirely by that greeting, Vivien was reduced to gaping at Lucca in bewilderment. 'But you know why I'm here!'

An aristocratic ebony brow ascended in polite disagreement, for he had exquisite manners. 'How could I know?'

'You sent me that newspaper,' Vivien reminded him rather tautly, for her extreme nervous tension was being heightened by an awful sense of foolishness.

Lucca shifted a fluid brown hand and spread dismissive fingers in a tiny, almost infinitesimal movement. *'So?'*

Vivien tried and failed to swallow past the lump lodged in her throat. 'Naturally I came straight here to see you.'

Lucca vented a soft, amused laugh that nonetheless contrived to create a chill somewhere deep down inside Vivien. 'Naturally? Would you care to explain how this sudden uninvited visit of yours could possibly be described as natural?'

Recognising the dangerous tension in the atmosphere, Vivien was daunted. Her own nature was too open for her to comprehend Lucca's darker and infinitely more complex temperament. She considered their meeting of overwhelming importance. His cool detachment disorientated her. 'It's like you're not really listening to me. Don't be like that, don't act like this is a game in which the highest score wins!'

'Don't make assumptions, *cara*. You're not inside my head and can have no idea what I'm thinking.'

'I know that you have to be very, very angry with me—'

'No, you're wrong,' Lucca traded. 'Anger over a long haul is unproductive. Even dinosaurs move on eventually.'

Vivien was too wound up to hold back the frantic words bubbling to her lips. 'I know you hate me and have to blame me for everything that's gone wrong…and that's OK, only what I deserve,' she conceded humbly.

'Don't waste my time with this,' Lucca urged, cold as ice.

Vivien raised anguished green eyes to his lean, strong face and willed him to listen to her and recognise her sincerity. 'Sorry is a very inadequate word and may even be horribly aggravating in these circumstances but I *have* to say it—'

'Why?' Brilliant dark eyes lit by a tiny inner flame of gold rested on her in blatant challenge. 'I'm not interested in hearing your apologies.'

'You sent me that newspaper…' Vivien reminded him again, but this time half under her breath.

Lucca shrugged a wide shoulder in a gesture of magnificent disregard.

In the silence that stretched, Vivien sucked in a deep, shuddering breath and pressed on. 'You wanted me to know that I'd misjudged you. You wanted me to see the proof that you were innocent.'

'Or maybe I wanted to make you squirm,' Lucca suggested silkily. 'Or maybe my pride demanded I have the last word. Whatever my motivation, it's not important now.'

'Of course, it's important!' Vivien was no longer able to restrain her teeming emotions. 'Jasmine Bailey destroyed our marriage—'

'No,' Lucca slotted in with lethal quietness. 'All the honours of that achievement go to you. If you had trusted me, we would still be together.'

Vivien fell back a step as if he had struck her. He had stripped the facts down to their bones and reached his own cruelly straightforward baseline. 'It's not that simple.'

'I think it is.'

'But you *let* me leave you!' Vivien protested in desperation. 'How hard did you try to persuade me that that horrible woman was lying?'

'Guilty until proven innocent…is that how you rationalise what you did? You shifted the burden of proof back onto me. But there was no way I could prove that Bailey had concocted her story. I slept alone that night and every night during that week in the Med but only I can know that for a fact,' Lucca pointed out, wide sculpted mouth grim. 'Bimbos target rich men. You knew that when you married me. The first line of defence in our marriage should have been trust and you fell at the starting gate.'

'I might have had more trust if you had been more vigorous in your denials!' Vivien argued, half an octave higher in volume, for she was aghast at his complete lack of emotion and utterly crushed by his disinterest. 'But it seems that you were too proud to try and convince me that I'd made a mistake and misjudged you—'

His intense gaze flashed gold and veiled. 'Get a grip, *cara*. This visit is an embarrassment for us both and it gives me no pleasure to tell you that.'

'You won't let me say sorry, will you?' Vivien grasped unhappily.

She was so earnest, so straightforward, so disastrously naïve, Lucca acknowledged. She was asking for trouble, inviting it in by calling open season. When he had married her, he reflected bitterly, he had planned to protect her from every evil. It had never occurred to him that he would find himself exiled to the enemy camp and the only escape route would entail compromising his own ideals. Sunlight distracted him from his brooding introspection as he studied her upturned face. The fine-grained perfection of her creamy skin illuminated green eyes with the depth and clarity of jewels and a wide, soft, vulnerable mouth as juicy and inviting as a ripe cherry. His body reacted with infuriating immediacy and hardened.

Vivien connected unwarily with riveting black eyes that turned her bones to water. She felt hot, weak and dizzy, her physical response to his aggressive masculinity instant and familiar. Black lashes as lush as his infant son's snapped down over his gaze, narrowing them to a vibrant glimmer, and he stepped back with measured cool.

'I don't know why you've come to see me,' Lucca stated with a cutting lack of expression.

'Yes, you do…you know absolutely why!' Vivien reasoned tautly, cheeks hotly flushed with agonised self-consciousness. She was struggling to concentrate rather than cringe at the suspicion that he had noticed her humiliating reaction to his proximity.

'But possibly I don't wish to engage on that subject,' Lucca fenced in a tone as smooth as black velvet. 'Why don't you tell me instead how Marco is doing?'

Vivien blinked and then the tense anxiety etched on

her face was softened by the warm beginnings of a loving smile. 'He's doing wonderfully well…he learns everything so fast, you know—'

Even that hint of a smile increased Lucca's anger. 'No, I don't know.'

'Sorry?' Vivien didn't understand. She had hoped that talking about their son, currently the only shared element in their lives, might take some of the chill out of the atmosphere.

'I said that no, I don't know how fast Marco learns because I don't see enough of my son to make that kind of judgement. Obviously, he's always doing or saying something new and different by the time I see him again.'

Vivien shrank at that icy clarification. 'I suppose he must do.'

'Evidently, it hasn't occurred to you either that I also missed out entirely on his first smile, his first step and his first word.'

Over-sensitive tears lashed and stung the back of Vivien's eyes and she had to keep them very wide to prevent them from spilling out and betraying her.

'I suppose that I should count myself lucky that he seems to recognise me from one visit to the next,' Lucca completed with the same cold, flat intonation.

For the first time, Vivien was confronted by his bitterness where their child was concerned. In shock, she swallowed so hard she hurt her throat and had to look away until she had control of herself again. Understanding how he must have felt at being excluded and essentially left unaware of all the most important moments in his toddler son's life, how could she blame him for his hostility? It seemed beneath her to remark that he was talking like a much fonder father than she would ever have expected him to become. One of her least favourite recollections was Lucca's annoyance when she had fallen pregnant.

'I wish I knew what to say,' she began awkwardly.

'Not the overworked, ever-cheerful English cliché for the occasion...*please*,' Lucca derided. 'Perhaps it is now sinking in on you that, like most divorced couples, we don't have much to talk about.'

'We're not divorced yet—'

'As good as, *cara mia*,' Lucca contradicted with an insolent insouciance that flayed her to the bone. 'Before you leave—I'm sure you don't want to be late— is there anything else you wish to discuss?'

Feeling harassed and unable to get her thoughts into any kind of useful order and horrendously loaded with guilt and unbearable regret, Vivien recalled her reluctant promise to her sister.

'Money...' she said abruptly.

Lucca frowned in surprise.

Vivien turned a beetroot colour and shifted uneasily off one foot onto the other. 'I mean, I'm having a little trouble managing at present. I'm also well aware that it was my choice to accept only minimal financial assistance from you after we separated—'

'We didn't separate,' Lucca interposed. 'You walked out on our marriage.'

Vivien gritted her teeth together, for she did not require that reminder, nor did she wish to recall how very much she had once valued her ability to remain almost independent of his wealth. 'Situations change. I was supposed to be writing a book this year and the department agreed to let me reduce my hours as a tutor. Unfortunately, the publisher decided the subject was too esoteric for the general public and pulled out.

I won't be able to return to full-time work in the botany department until the next academic year.'

'I gather you had no contract with the publisher...'

Vivien nodded grudging confirmation and wondered how on earth she had let herself be persuaded into discussing something so remote from the emotions surging through her in great waves of frustrated grief.

'My lawyers will contact yours and work out an appropriate arrangement. It's not a problem. Did you think it would be a problem? Is that why you took the opportunity to approach me with fervent apologies today?' Lucca demanded in a sudden switch of subject that caught her quite unprepared.

Vivien dealt him a startled glance. 'Of course, it isn't—'

'Perhaps you thought I would be a mean bastard and refuse to step into the breach?' Lucca flashed her a shimmering look of contempt.

'No, I didn't think that!' But her pride, she was willing to admit, had shrunk from the prospect of admitting just how much she now needed the monetary help that she had once declined.

'In spite of the fact that I was not the guilty party in the breakdown of our marriage, I was never petty. It was you who threw *my* generosity back in my face,' Lucca condemned with harsh emphasis. 'Although it was my right to contribute to my son's upkeep, your selfish intransigence prevented me from advancing more than a tiny sum.'

Beneath that onslaught, Vivien had grown so pale and tense that her fine facial bones were clearly delineated by her pale skin. 'I had no idea you felt like that about supporting Marco.'

His handsome jaw line squared to an aggressive angle. Again he shrugged, cold eyes black as polished jet dismissing her as a creature of no import. '*Dio mio.* Why should you have? Our only communication since you left has been through lawyers. Do you want a cheque now?'

Vivien reddened as though he had slapped her and pure anguish filled her, forming a tight, hard, intolerable knot somewhere below her ribs. Was he willing to do or say anything to get rid of her? 'No…that's truly not why I came to see you, Lucca.'

'Yet a mercenary motive makes more sense than any other,' Lucca fielded with supreme scorn 'You're lucky you can't be prosecuted for embarrassing me—'

'Embarrassing you?'

'As ex-wives go you look very poor and my enemies must think I keep a very tight hold on my cash reserves.'

'I don't *have* a mercenary motive!' Vivien protested in growing consternation at his attitude. 'Is it so hard for you to accept that I was and still am genuinely devastated by what Jasmine Bailey confessed in that newspaper today?'

Lucca elevated a brow. 'No, I can accept that. Which of us enjoys being proven wrong? However, I really cannot understand why you felt the need to share your reaction with me in person.'

Vivien breathed in jerkily. 'You *don't*…?'

'We're virtually divorced—'

'We're not…stop saying that!'

'But our marriage is over, dead, buried so deep it will never see the light of day again except on our son's birth certificate,' Lucca extended, his honeyed drawl thick with raw, biting derision. 'Wake up and stop playing the Sleeping Beauty, who's been stood up by the Prince. Two years have gone by. I hardly remember my time with you. It's not even as though we were together that long.'

Every word was like a dagger plunged between Vivien's ribs, poisoned and deadly, slicing in fast and hurting her more than she could bear. Part of her wanted to scream at him in tormented rebuttal but the other part of her wanted to curl up and die somewhere dark and silent and private. Every single memory of that same period they had been together remained as fresh as yesterday to her. It might have ended in tears but she had not allowed herself to become bitter and she had cherished the special memories she still had. In comparison, Lucca was telling her what no woman wanted to hear: he was spelling out the reality that theirs had only been one relationship amongst many in his past and he had moved on. Had it been two years? How had she contrived to overlook just how much time had passed?

Vivien looked peaky enough to be on the brink of fainting and her transparent pallor pierced the deep polar freeze with which Lucca had encased his responses. Had he set out to be deliberately cruel? He did not think so. He had only told her the truth, only pointed out that her behaviour was unwise and irrational. Even so, he asked her to sit down and when she refused offered her a drink.

'I don't...' she muttered and looked fixedly down at her watch in an attempt to reinstate her self-discipline because inside herself she felt incredibly bruised and sensitive.

'Yes, I know that, but perhaps just this once you could take a brandy,' Lucca suggested rather curtly, disliking the tenor of his own concern. 'When did you last remember to eat?'

'Breakfast.'

He said nothing. She did not stop to eat when she was involved in anything that absorbed her concentration. He remembered the way his staff used to look after her in his absence, serving meals on trays when she was deep in her research and producing finger foods when her appetite needed tempting. She was extremely clever when it came to the rare plants she studied but not by any stretch of the imagination a woman of a practical bent.

Vivien lifted her head, green eyes haunted by the spectres of the past she had had and lost again. 'You don't want me to express my very great regret because you can't forgive me,' she whispered tightly. 'I understand that and right now I don't think I'll ever forgive myself.'

Taken aback by the intensity she exuded, Lucca pressed the brandy he had poured into her taut grasp. 'I'll call a limo for you. Did you travel here by train?'

'Yes, but I don't need a limo.' She tipped the crystal glass to her lips, let the alcohol burn a fiery passage down past her dry and aching throat and pool like molten fire in the hollow pit of her tummy. While he watched with increasing fascination, she gulped the brandy down as though it were a soft drink and walked to the door. She was so deep in her own thoughts that she bumped into a chair and had to steady herself on it with one hand.

'I insist that you wait for a limo to take you to the station,' Lucca decreed.

'I don't listen when you insist any more.' Vivien held her fair head high on her slender neck and her slight shoulders hurt with the tension of her rigid carriage.

Our marriage is over, dead, buried so deep it will never see the light of day again.

'Vivi…be sensible.'

The use of that affectionate abbreviation of her name hurt like the sting of a bee, at first only a sharp, tiny, needling sensation that would ultimately be followed by greater pain. Her lovely face pale but seemingly serene, she walked out through the reception area and stepped into the sanctuary of the lift, horribly ill at ease beneath the prying, curious eyes trained on her. Already she was remembering other occasions when Lucca had called her by that name.

'Vivi…don't nag,' he would reprove when she had endeavoured to persuade him to aim at spending one evening a week with her. An evening that would just be for them, not a night when they socialised with others or a night when he worked so late that she fell asleep alone in their bed. 'Quality time is what you save for children and thankfully we don't have any yet.'

'Vivi…the scent of your skin drives me wild,' he used to groan, kissing her awake with the seductive expertise for which he was famed and, even though she had so often been tired and sad, the only earthly paradise she had ever known had been the magic she had discovered in his arms.

'Vivi…life will be so sweet for you now that you have me,' he had promised with dazzling confidence and conviction on their wedding night and she had blindly trusted and believed it would be exactly as he'd said it would be.

The lift came to a halt and jolted Vivien back to the

present and the noise and bustle of the busy ground floor. On the street, she caught a glimpse of her own ghostly reflection in a shop window and a laugh that was no laugh at all was torn from her.

Typically, it had not even occurred to her to think about her own appearance. When she had left Lucca, she had decided that such frivolous considerations were no longer necessary. But now she was aghast at her pale, plain reflection and the deeply unsexy baggy silhouette of her linen top and skirt. She should have dressed up for Lucca's benefit. Perhaps he would have listened then. An Italian to the backbone, from the skin out he exuded designer elegance.

Someone collided with her and cannoned away again. 'Why don't you look where you're going?' an angry woman demanded, pushing past with the toddler who had smeared his ice-cream cone across Vivien's skirt.

'Signora Saracino…?'

Vivien looked across the pavement in surprise. Lucca's chauffeur, Roberto, was holding open the passenger door of a long, gleaming limousine parked by the kerb. People walking past were looking at her. Colouring, she wondered just how long she had been standing staring at herself in the window and if indeed she was behaving as oddly as she felt. The suspicion was sufficient to persuade her that accepting a lift was the lesser of two evils.

Our marriage is over, dead, buried so deep it will never see the light of day again.

For goodness' sake, why couldn't she get those words out of her head? A sense of deep humiliation drenched her. Bernice had been aghast when Vivien had announced that she needed to see Lucca. Now it was obvious that she should have taken heed of her worldlier sibling's opinion. Lucca had been cold, derisive and hostile. He had not shown the smallest interest in anything she'd had to say but had been reasonably enthusiastic about encouraging her departure. He had accused her of embarrassing them both. Anyone would think she had burst through his office door shouting that she still loved him and wanted him back! *As if…* Mouth tight to stop it quivering, pained eyes burning, Vivien snatched in a jagged breath.

It was almost impossible to recall that little more than three years ago. Lucca had acted as though she were a glittering prize to be won. Back then, he had seemed far from indifferent and it had taken him weeks just to persuade her to give him a chance…

The first Vivien had known of Lucca's earthly existence was when he'd pinched her reserved parking space while she'd been painstakingly lining up her car to reverse into it. Having read about people who died in road rage attacks, she'd fumed in silence while she'd searched the busy campus for another place to park. Walking past that stolen space, she'd glowered unimpressed at the opulent scarlet Ferrari, which had already gathered a clutch of youthful male admirers.

Her bad day had not improved. Before she'd even got her coat off, a colleague had informed her that a visiting VIP was using her office to make his phone calls.

'So what am I supposed to do?' Vivien groaned because she had work to do and wanted to get on with it. 'Who is it?'

'Lucca Saracino…probably the most influential businessman who ever graduated from this institution,' the older man explained. 'He is so rich that that Ferrari parked out there could be fuelled on liquid gold and he's thinking about endowing the faculty with a new research facility. We're lucky he wasn't offered the whole building for his private use!'

'Saracino...' Vivien repeated, for the name was vaguely familiar. 'I have a student called Serafina Saracino—'

'His kid sister is here on a year's exchange,' her companion confirmed.

Vivien defrosted a little and waited outside her own office with greater patience. At the start of term, Serafina had been extremely homesick and had tearfully confided in Vivien, who had become fond of the younger woman.

'Why?' a male drawl queried with a definable foreign accent, making Vivien peer at the door of her office, which stood ajar. 'There *is* no reason why, Elaine. We've had fun together but time moves on and so must I. I'm not into fidelity or the long-term factor.'

Vivien flinched. Some poor woman was getting dumped by an arrogant louse with a lump of concrete where his heart should be. She was about to move out of hearing distance when the head of her department, Professor Anstey, appeared with a very bored-looking blonde by his side. Three things then happened simultaneously. A very tall dark male emerged from Vivien's office. Suddenly energised, the blonde surged forward to cling possessively to his arm and whisper in a breathy intimate undertone. At the same time, the professor stepped forward to introduce Vivien.

'Dr Dillon...' Lucca Saracino murmured after a perceptible pause, his accent very pronounced.

'Mr Saracino...' Vivien looked up into a face of

such breathtaking male beauty that momentarily all thought was suspended. The long-lashed brilliance of his black eyes seemed to reach inside her and cut off her ability to breathe at source. For a shameful instant, she was unaware of anything but him.

But then his lovely lady friend literally stepped between them. Vivien recognised her own brief lapse in concentration with a shock of recoil that made her freeze. Lucca Saracino was a very rich and very arrogant womaniser, in every way the sort of male she avoided. He attempted to extend their dialogue but her eyes would no longer meet his and her responses were as discouraging as her stance. With a harried reference to the time, she escaped into her office.

Two days later, she was giving a lecture based on the textbook she had written on ferns while she was still a student and she almost succumbed to nervous panic when she saw Lucca Saracino in the back row. Afterwards, he was waiting with his sister Serafina to invite her out to lunch and Vivien tried to make a gracious refusal.

'Please...' the bubbly brunette pressed with determination. 'Everybody knows how shy you are but Lucca only wants to thank you for letting me wail all over you when I was so unhappy.'

'Untrue. I would like to enjoy the simple pleasure of your company, Dr Dillon,' Lucca contradicted, stunning dark eyes making her mouth run dry and her tummy flip.

Reluctant to hurt his sister's feelings, Vivien acquiesced. Over the meal, she barely touched her food while Lucca planted subtle personal questions that she did not have the conversational dexterity to avoid answering.

Afterwards, Serafina rushed off to a lecture and, when Vivien attempted to imitate that fast exit, Lucca said with a mixture of amusement and faint annoyance, 'Why have you decided not to like me?'

'Where on earth did you get that idea?' Vivien protested, writhing in embarrassment at the depth of his insight.

Yet in truth she did not know what to say to him or even what she was feeling. There was no way she would have confessed to a living soul and least of all him that from the moment she first saw him she had not existed a minute without thinking of him in some way. He was a stranger and yet he was not. In that initial fleeting meeting some connection had been forged that she could not shake off.

He asked her out to dinner, the date to be of her choosing so that she could not fall back on the excuse of pleading a prior engagement. She was astonished by that expression of personal interest on his part because she had simply assumed that the wicked attraction he exuded for her was a one-sided thing.

'I think you are very beautiful,' Lucca informed her with the enjoyment of a male who could read her mind.

'I'm not at all beautiful!' Vivien argued, defiant in her conviction that she was being fed a nonsensical line. Assuring him quite truthfully that she didn't date and less truthfully that there was nothing personal in her lack of interest, she fled.

Every day after that, for two entire weeks, he sent her the most beautiful flowers, wonderful imaginative offerings that went far beyond standard bouquets. On the third weekend, Lucca arrived at her small apartment with dinner in a picnic basket. He charmed his way into her home and with glorious cool served them both with a gorgeous meal. Only when he was leaving did he ask her out again.

'You're crazy,' she muttered in despair at his utterly single-minded pursuit. 'Why would someone like you even want to go out with me?'

'I can't think about anything else.'

'That doesn't make sense.'

'You can't think of anything else either.' Lucca delivered that *coup de grâce* without hesitation. 'What has sense to do with this?'

But for Vivien sense had everything to do with it. She did not chase rainbows and she always respected her own limitations. She knew that she was useless with men and she was far too cautious to give her heart to someone who would treat it and her like a football once he had got bored. Yes, it hurt almost intolerably to deny her helpless craving to be with him, but to have him and lose him again would be much worse. So she laughed in the face of his boundless confidence, unwilling to acknowledge that he was right on target.

He began phoning her, but only occasionally. She began waiting for his calls and was disappointed and unable to settle when they didn't come. On the phone she found him endlessly entertaining without being threatening and she continued to deny the growing strength of her own feelings. Meanwhile her peace of mind evaporated and her once total absorption in her work vanished. She had no idea that Lucca was steadily breaking down her defences until she dropped into Serafina's leaving party in the summer term and saw him with another woman. Literally torn apart by the most violent sense of betrayal, she was finally forced to confront the power of her emotional attachment to Lucca Saracino...

Emerging from that energising recollection of the past into the even more challenging present, Vivien registered that once again she was in a very similar position. She gazed out the windows of the limo and saw nothing. Exactly what *were* her feelings for her husband? As soon as she had read Jasmine Bailey's confession, she had dropped everything in her urgent need to see Lucca. It was true that honour demanded that she immediately make every effort to express her regret for not having had greater faith in him two years earlier. But was that really the only reason she had fired off like a rocket to London?

Vivien found herself squirming at that inner question but she made herself answer it truthfully. And the answer was so self-serving she was thoroughly ashamed of herself. The instant the barrier of Lucca's supposed infidelity had been swept from her path, she had wanted him back. Without the smallest forethought she had approached him in the desperate hope of saving their marriage before the divorce went through. Wasn't that what her real motivation had been? Hopefully Lucca remained in blissful ignorance of her foolish secret hopes. So did that mean she just went back home because he had told her to go back home? Was that it? Had she really made her best effort?

She found herself striving to remember how many rejections Lucca had swallowed before she'd finally surrendered and agreed to go out with him. Lucca was very proud yet, three years ago, he had persisted in spite of her rebuffs. It would have been so much easier for Lucca to walk away and choose one of the many women who would have been flattered by his interest and immediately responsive. But Lucca had decided that he wanted her and he had not let pride get in the way of that objective.

Vivien straightened her bent spine as though someone had jabbed a well-aimed hat-pin into a tender part of her anatomy. At the first taste of embarrassment and hurt pride, she had been ready to give up. Shame enveloped her. Just three short years ago, Lucca had fought for her…did she have the courage to fight for him? And for their marriage? Was she prepared to ditch her pride and make the effort to persuade Lucca that their marriage could still have a chance? It did not take much time for her to make a decision: existing without Lucca was like being only half alive.

The limousine was already drawing into the station to drop her off and she clambered out for want of anything better to do. Noticing the ice-cream stains on her skirt, which she had forgotten, she groaned. She would have to buy a change of clothes before she could make a second call on Lucca, who had long since impressed her with the reality that whether she approved or otherwise, people made value judgements on the basis of appearance.

It took some time for her to find her way back to an area where she was familiar with the shops and it took even longer for her to locate a suitable outfit. Stiff with reluctance, for she absolutely loathed wearing anything that attracted the least attention to her person, Vivien chose an ice-blue dress. Lucca had always preferred to see her clothed in light, bright colours. Letting the pale golden weight of her hair fall loose round her shoulders, she brushed it smooth.

She took a taxi to the elegant residential square

where Lucca now owned a Georgian townhouse. His interior designer had sold illicit pictures to a glossy magazine and Bernice had drawn her sister's attention to the article. It seemed especially ironic to Vivien that Lucca should finally have given up the vast minimalist apartment that she had loathed only *after* their marriage had broken down.

Her body taut with tension, she climbed out of the taxi with thoughts that were wholly dominated by the enervating challenge of what she should say to Lucca. Someone shouted her name and, when she glanced up in surprise, a man with a camera took a picture of her and urged her to stay where she was to enable him to take another. At the same time other people were running across the road towards her, shouting questions. For a split second she was so taken aback by the onslaught, she was paralysed to the spot, and then she dropped her head and raced as fast as she could up the steps to ring the bell on Lucca's front door.

The paparazzi crowded round her in a suffocating crush. 'How do you feel about Jasmine Bailey now, Mrs Saracino?'

'You were seen at your husband's office this afternoon.' A microphone was thrust in Vivien's stricken face and more cameras clicked. 'Is it true that Lucca made you wait for hours before he would agree to see you?'

'Are you aware that Lucca is currently seeing Bliss Masterson? She's one of the most beautiful women in the world. How does that make you feel? Do you find that intimidating?' Horrified by the shocking intrusiveness of that cruel interrogation, and backed up against the door in her desperate desire to escape, Vivien could easily have fallen when the door opened abruptly. Happily, a strong arm braced her and lifted her smoothly over the threshold.

'Vivien…are you trying to save your marriage?' the last reporter screeched like a vulture just before the door thudded shut.

'Are you all right?' Wearing an expression of concern, her rescuer urged her down into a chair in the huge gracious hall. It was Arlo, Lucca's Chief of Security, who had always been very kind to her

'F-fine…' Vivien stammered, her teeth chattering together while she struggled to still the tremors of shock still coursing through her slender body.

'That's good, *cara*.' Another, infinitely less sympathetic voice interposed from several feet away. 'I would hate to be deprived of the opportunity of telling you that coming here tonight has to be the stupidest thing you have ever done!'

CHAPTER THREE

AGHAST at that condemnation, Vivien focused on Lucca as he strode towards her. The sight of him transfixed her and slashed like a cruel blade through her concentration. She, who had always liked to argue that looks were a superficial thing and not half so important as intellect and personality, was utterly dazzled by Lucca's raw masculine vibrancy. He was so gorgeous that just looking at his lean, strong face and hard, powerful body made her feel dizzy and weak.

'How on earth can you say that?' Vivien fumbled and found those words with difficulty and rose hurriedly up from the chair to defend herself. Lucca would steamroller over her and verbally pound her into submission if she did not fight back.

'It was obvious that the press would pounce at the first sign that you were reacting to the Bailey woman's confession!' Lucca proclaimed, his anger given a keener edge by the shocked pallor of fright that she still wore.

'I was so wound up by all this,' Vivien admitted ruefully with the frankness that was a great part of her charm, 'that I'm afraid that that risk just didn't occur to me.'

'But it should've done.' Lucca was too exasperated to be softened by the genuine regret clouding her lovely green eyes. Tomorrow the newspapers would carry unflattering photos of her clad like a tiny fragile ghost in a very strange wispy dress with fluttering sleeves and a fussy handkerchief hem. A fashion accident of pile-up proportions, it had most probably leapt right off the hanger into Vivien's appreciative arms.

'Yes…do you think I could have a drink?' Vivien enquired in an apologetic undertone, for she was still feeling distinctly unsteady on her feet. But then it was hardly surprising that she should feel faint when she had not eaten since breakfast-time, she conceded ruefully. Recalling the restorative powers of the brandy she had imbibed in Lucca's office, she decided to temporarily set aside her objections to alcohol and make use of it on what was a momentous occasion.

Another drink? Lucca was startled by her request and hugely disapproving. Had she begun drinking since their separation? He thrust wide the door of an imposing reception room decorated in cool shades of blue.

Vivien fiddled with one trailing sleeve, hands so restless she wished she could fold them up and put them away. 'I know you have to be wondering why I've come back to see you…'

'You couldn't find you way back to the train?'

Chagrined colour laced her tense pallor and her chin came up. 'This is serious—'

'*Sì…*' A slanting smile that was somehow an insult formed on Lucca's beautifully moulded mouth as he extended a brandy goblet. 'Here we are practically divorced and all of a sudden you're in my face. Quite unexpectedly, I'm very much in demand. You say this is serious. Is it?'

Vivien stood very straight, green eyes strained. 'Please don't be like this…I don't know how to get through to you when you're in this kind of mood.'

Lucca sent her a shimmering glance, dense black lashes low over dangerous golden eyes. 'Perhaps if you had known that this day would come you might have acted differently during our separation—'

'If I had had foreknowledge of that hateful woman's confession today, there would never have *been* a separation!' Vivien protested with strong feeling.

'Two years ago you took a stranger's word over mine and that was the end of our marriage,' Lucca fenced back, cold as ice that burned.

Frantic though Vivien was to remind him of just how things had been between them at the time, she was afraid to add fuel to the flames of his hostility. 'There was a distance between us then...you know there was. We hardly saw each other those last weeks. You were in New York, then you were on the yacht—'

'You could have been with me,' Lucca slotted in lethally.

Vivien knotted her restless hands together and then moved them apart in a gesture of frustration. 'You worked such long hours—'

'I warned you about that when I married you,' Lucca interposed crushingly.

'I had to have my studies to keep me busy. Lucca, please give me your whole attention for a couple of minutes so that I can say what I need to say,' Vivien pleaded.

Lucca contrived to look eaten alive with boredom without either speaking or moving a muscle.

Her fingers knotted tight by her sides. 'I made a mistake...a hideous, horrible mistake and I admit that. I also understand that you're very angry.'

Lucca parted perfect masculine lips.

'Shut up...don't say anything!' Vivien hurried into

adding. 'I know I have a lot of making up to do and
that sorry doesn't cover it. But I also know that when
I was with you I was happier than I had ever been in
my life before.'

Lucca expelled his breath in a slow measured hiss
of self-restraint. How was he supposed to believe that?

High spots of pink bloomed over Vivien's taut
cheekbones. 'I would do just about anything to get that
happiness back.'

Anger flared like distant lightning in his steady scrutiny. 'You had it and you threw it away again, *cara*.
What you're feeling now is not my problem.'

Vivien flinched. His dark-as-night eyes were hard
as diamonds that cut glass. But although innate caution
urged her to cut and run before she spelt out her intentions any more clearly, she could not bear to remain
silent. The least she owed him was her honesty. 'I
accept that...but I've also learned a lot about myself
in the last few hours. I haven't been happy since I left
you.'

'That's sad, but good to know,' Lucca confided
without a shade of remorse, remembering how she had
looked on their Tuscan honeymoon: adoring green
eyes full of joy, soft full mouth curved into a shy smile
of contentment. An intimate recollection of her slim,
eager body splayed across linen sheets followed and
ignited his all-male libido.

Vivien collided with brilliant eyes as dark as jet.
When the darkness of his intent gaze suddenly flamed
gold, her heart lurched as though Lucca had aimed a
kick at it. Her breath trapped in her dry throat, she
stared back, her heartbeat pounding behind her ribs,
her slight figure held taut with unbearable tension. She
felt as if she were standing on the edge of a precipice,

only the fear that gripped her was also laced with helpless longing. The desire she had made herself forget
during their separation had flared up again inside her
as though someone had tossed a flaming torch on a
bale of hay.

Her voice emerged husky and breathless as she
forced herself to concentrate long enough to say what
she knew she needed to say. 'I still have feelings for
you and I'm asking you to give our marriage another
chance. I want you back.'

Intense satisfaction of the darkest kind engulfed
Lucca when he was already on an angry high of lust.
'You want me back?'

So tense that her muscles were hurting, Vivien
jerked her chin in affirmation. 'Yes. I want you back,'
she repeated, fighting to remain unbowed by his lack
of reaction, fighting not to feel diminished by her own
humble admission.

The buzz of fierce sexual awareness had thickened
the atmosphere.

'It's not mutual,' Lucca delivered, studying her ripe
full mouth with fixed attention.

The rage locked inside him had expanded and was
now threatening to explode. It had been a long time
since he was that angry. Two years, in fact. Two years
since his marriage had crashed and burned. Two years
since she had sacrificed their relationship and their future child's security with a resolute determination that
had shattered his expectations of his once adoring little
wife.

'But you could think about it...' Vivien persisted
unevenly.

'I don't need to *think* about it!' Lucca bit out in
raw, harsh dismissal.

Trembling and striving to conceal her anguish, Vivien dropped her head.

'On the other hand,' Lucca grated, 'while our marriage was a mistake—'

'Don't say that,' she urged, appalled by that brutal declaration given without hesitation as though it were established fact.

'I still wouldn't throw you out of bed...'

Totally taken aback by that unanticipated completion and unable to immediately understand it, Vivien looked up, the tip of her tongue snaking out to wet her dry lower lip. 'Sorry...?'

With the expertise of a male to whom no move was a challenge around a woman, Lucca reached out and closed his arms round her slight figure to propel her forward and demonstrate his meaning with action. Vivien blinked up at him like a mesmerised owl. He bound her to him with strong hands and plundered her ripe mouth with a hot, hard sexual intensity that smashed down her every barrier.

Reeling from the surprise of that passionate onslaught, she swayed. Clamping her to the hard, muscular heat of his lean, powerful frame, he backed her up against the wall behind her.

'Lucca...' she mumbled unsteadily with no thought of resisting him, for he never, ever talked about feelings and had always used his raw sexuality as a means of communication. So, when he touched her again for the first time in two years, she believed she had broken through his barriers and that he was accepting her back into his life.

'Want me?' he growled.

'Always...'

In answer he kissed her as though he were devour-

ing her. It was incredibly sexy. Her head swam and
her lungs burned from lack of oxygen, but she held
him to her with eager, greedy hands. Mad excitement
and joy were coursing through her in a seductive tidal
wave. Her body was molten liquid in response, flaming with the feverish heat she had never dreamt she
would feel again. A dulled, nagging ache pulsed at the
very heart of her, making her shift forward into instinctive closer contact.

An almost imperceptible shudder ran through
Lucca's big, powerful frame. He wanted to lift her up
against him and sink into the tight, sweet promise of
her tiny body again and again and again until he had
finally sated the blaze of blistering desire that inflamed
him. But in the room next door another woman was
waiting for him. A woman, he reminded himself dog-
gedly, whom he could take without fuss or promises
or complications. A split second later, however, he
reached a decision. There was no reason why he
should not celebrate his approaching freedom by taking his soon-to-be ex-wife back to his bed one more
time purely to demonstrate just what she had care-
lessly thrown away...

Closing his lean brown hands over Vivien's slim,
clinging arms, he urged them down from his shoulders
to her sides and forced a little space between them.
'This is not good timing for me.'

Her glowing eyes clung to his lean, darkly handsome features. She could not conceal her dizzy happiness. 'What does timing have to do with anything?
I just want to be with you.'

Brilliant dark eyes shimmering, Lucca stilled.
Outrage filled him. How could she think for one moment that it would be that easy to get him back? He

would never forgive her. He was finished with her. Had she honestly believed that all she had to do was say sorry and they would kiss and make up like little kids after a childish argument? If she thought that, she was out of her mind! Cold, dark fury ran like bars of steel through Lucca and, at his coldest, he was also at his most merciless.

'I think we could be talking at cross purposes, *cara*,' Lucca murmured very drily. 'I'm not interested in re-instating our former marriage. How many times do I have to tell you that that's out of the question and very much in the past?'

Vivien had fallen as still as an accident victim. The colour was slowly draining from her delicate pointed face, leaving her waxen pale. She felt like someone trying to wade blindfolded through a swamp because she could not understand why he should suddenly be studying her as though she were a rather pathetic spec-imen under a lab scope. 'But only thirty seconds ago, you were…you were k-kissing me,' she stammered in bewilderment.

Lucca watched her and almost winced. She was so literal, so straightforward, seeing black and white and no shades of grey. Around him, she was an accident waiting to happen. That awareness only increased his anger. The blame for their wrecked marriage was hers, not his.

'That was sex,' he told her with cruel casualness.

Predictably, Vivien reddened and made restive movements, that three-letter word being one that she was always ludicrously keen to avoid. 'Obviously, yes…but—'

'I can fancy a quick tumble without any desire to embrace holy matrimony again,' Lucca filled in with derisive cool. 'As I recall, you were surprisingly hot between the sheets.'

At that unsought accolade, calculated to underline her loss of dignity, Vivien slapped him so hard her wrist went numb. She felt no shame or regret either. She would not allow him to speak to her like that. Hopefully too he would remember being slapped longer than he would remember her pitifully immediate surrender to his first contemptuous kiss. White as death, but her narrow spine rigid and her green eyes unseeing, she sidestepped him. She must not, could not allow herself to break down and make an even bigger fool of herself in his presence.

'No woman has ever dared to hit me before...' Hard jaw line squared, Lucca stepped in front of her to prevent her fast walk in the direction of the door.

'It shows,' Vivien told him half under her breath, striving not to let her evasive gaze come to rest on the angry red imprint of her fingers across one smooth, hard Latin cheekbone. 'Whatever I did in the past, and however much I've annoyed you today, I had good intentions and no wish to hurt or offend. I don't deserve to be spoken to as though I'm the dirt below your feet—'

'I didn't—'

'Nor will I allow you to make me feel ashamed of trying to save our marriage—'

'But you didn't bloody well try for five minutes two years ago!' Lucca slung back with an icy condemnation that stopped Vivien in her tracks.

She was already fighting to contain the anguish inside her. She had lost him finally and for ever. There was to be no going back, no second chance. He despised her. And could she really blame him?

Everything that had gone wrong, it seemed, was solely her fault. Only, even in the midst of her utter misery, she knew that that was not strictly true. She might have been much happier with him than she had been without him but their marriage had been far from perfect and any compromises made had been hers alone.

'Perhaps it is too late but I'm trying now,' she countered painfully. 'Is that such a crime?'

Without any warning the door opened and a very tall, striking brunette appeared on the threshold.

'Bliss…I'm almost finished,' Lucca murmured smooth as glass. 'I'll be with you in a few minutes.'

Bliss? Bliss Masterson? Vivien had not recognised that name when it had been hurled at her by the paparazzi, but she did recognise that fabulous face from the marketing campaign in which the supermodel posed as a warrior princess to sell exotic perfume.

Like a mouse charmed by a deadly cobra, Vivien found herself staring at the most beautiful woman in the world. She couldn't help staring because Bliss *was* gorgeous enough to stop traffic. Hair the colour of polished jet fell straight and smooth as silk framing perfect features and turquoise eyes. The brunette was slim and shapely and extremely elegant. Vivien's heart sank as she realised that the whole time she had been with Lucca, Bliss must have been waiting for him. While Vivien had been engaged in her desperate clumsy struggle to persuade Lucca to give their marriage and her another chance, Lucca must have been wishing her a world away.

'Vivien…' With enviable social poise, Bliss glided gracefully forward. 'We haven't met before but I feel I know you already through your son.'

'My son…?' Vivien felt sick with mortification.

'Marco is so delightful…and very like his father.' Bliss sent an intimate smile in Lucca's direction. 'I just adore children.'

'Yes,' Vivien mumbled, ducking her head to hide the anguished strain in her eyes. She felt horribly out of place and humiliated not only by the other woman's presence, but also by Bliss's unexpected familiarity with Marco. Appreciating that she herself was the un-invited guest only made Vivien feel worse.

Bliss seemed very much at home in Lucca's town-house and quite unruffled by the appearance of Lucca's wife. Vivien's throat tightened. Would Lucca tell Bliss that Vivien had begged him for a second chance? Would they share a pitying laugh about her? Compared with Bliss Masterson…but how could she possibly compare to such a woman? She was small and fair and imperfect in every way. Even her hide-ously expensive new dress looked stupid next to the brunette's simple cream shift!

Tears burning the back of her eyes, Vivien headed towards the door that led back out into the hall.

'You should wait,' Lucca informed her. 'We don't want to create another media frenzy. Bliss should leave first by the rear entrance. She's running late for a charity event.'

Entrapped, Vivien hovered and fought to keep a lid on her distress while also maintaining a fake smile on a mouth that felt as though it had been carved out of wood. Being forced to tolerate the sight of Lucca with Bliss affected Vivien like a dagger plunged to the hilt in her heart. Mercifully, Lucca escorted the exquisite model from the room.

'I do hope we meet again,' Bliss bubbled sweetly on her way past.

Vivien closed her hands together in an effort to stop them trembling. Why the heck had she come back to see Lucca? What madness had possessed her? When had Lucca ever been free of female company? What price courage now?

The mobile phone in her bag rang and, numbly, she dug it out to answer it.

'Where are you?' Fabian Garsdale enquired thinly. 'I've been waiting for almost half an hour.'

'Oh, Fabian…' Guilt engulfed Vivien, for only now was she remembering that she had agreed to attend an evening lecture with the older man while his mother minded Marco. The arrangement had been made weeks earlier and Mrs Garsdale would be justifiably offended by so belated a cancellation. 'I'm so, so sorry…something came up. How can I excuse myself? I totally forgot we were supposed to be going out to-night!'

In the doorway, Lucca came to a sudden halt. It took a great deal to disconcert Lucca, but that latter snatch of overheard dialogue achieved the feat. He levelled startled dark eyes on Vivien's delicate profile. She had acted so innocent. She had even talked as if she still cared about him. Indeed, just a few minutes ago, she had fallen into his arms with alacrity. Yet, in spite of all that, Vivien had another man in her life. Lucca was outraged by that revelation. Fabian? What a deeply creepy name! Probably some boring nerd built like a stick insect, a smug, bookish weed more at home in the library than the bedroom, Lucca decided with sardonic distaste.

Unaware that she had an audience, Vivien was wincing with regret at her lack of tact in admitting that she had forgotten her arrangement with Fabian. 'I had better call your mother personally and apologise…after she made such a generous offer to help out too.'

'I've already informed Mother that you've been taken ill, so there's no need to call this evening.'

Vivien was relieved that Fabian sounded mollified by her response.

Lucca went rigid at the revelation that Vivien's relationship evidently extended to an acquaintance with the nerd's mother. So it was *that* serious. *Dio mio*…could that mean that Vivien, the last of the twentieth-century puritans, was actually sharing a bed with the guy? Lucca was disgusted, one hundred per cent disgusted, and sincerely appalled at that unexpected fall in Vivien's very high moral standards. Certainly he did not begrudge Vivien the right to lead her own life. However, Marco's needs had to come first and Lucca did not consider what he perceived to be the threat of a stepfather to be in his son's best interests.

'Did Bernice tell you where I am?' Vivien asked Fabian uncomfortably.

'Bernice isn't here. There are lights on but there doesn't seem to be anyone at home.'

Vivien was very surprised to hear that. Bernice would have had to get Marco out of bed to go out anywhere and, once wakened, Marco was not easily settled again. She frowned and then caught sight of Lucca.

'Talking on mobile phones is very expensive,' Fabian complained.

Bang, bang, bang went Vivien's heart while she stared at Lucca's lean bronzed features and she cringed for herself. How could she still be so susceptible? What a very sad individual she must seem to Lucca and his breathtakingly hip girlfriend! Poor, lonely Vivien, chasing romantic rainbows two years too late and a husband who believed their entire marriage had been a ghastly mistake!

Painfully conscious of Lucca's dark, glittering appraisal, and convinced that he was embarrassed by her inability to match his cool attitude, Vivien forced another false smile onto her down-curved lips. With as near an approximation of a chirpy giggle as she could manage, she told Fabian that she would see him when she got back.

'I'll look into your office on Friday…two can eat as cheaply as one!' Fabian was dropping a heavy hint that he was hoping to share her packed lunch. She almost laughed out loud, and was then ashamed of herself, for Fabian might be a little tight with money but he was also a colleague worthy of her respect and had proven himself to be a kind and reliable friend.

Refusing to look back in Lucca's direction, for her self-discipline was stretched too thin over her turbulent emotions, Vivien put away her phone and murmured flatly, 'I'd better get going…'

'You can't leave.'

'Sorry?' Vivien sent Lucca a bemused glance.

'The house is surrounded by paparazzi. Bliss managed to slip away but we can't hope to pull off the same stunt twice in one evening,' Lucca spelt out drily. 'You'll have to stay the night and sneak out in the morning.'

Vivien studied him in dismay and set off regardless towards the front door. 'I couldn't possibly stay…that's out of the question.'

'The press are waiting out there for you,' Lucca

murmured silkily. 'Your arrival an hour ago only whet their appetite. They'll be even more aggressive second time round.'

Daunted by that warning, Vivien paled. 'I know, but I *can't* stay here—'

'Why not? It's the easy way out. The paparazzi won't wait all night and a discreet departure at an early hour tomorrow will take care of the problem.' Lean, powerful face cool, as though there were nothing more natural than offering hospitality to his unwelcome and soon-to-be divorced wife, Lucca dealt her an expectant appraisal.

Meeting his brilliant dark golden eyes, Vivien went pink and hurriedly tore her gaze from his. She did not wish to remain below his roof, but she had found the paparazzi distinctly intimidating and what Lucca said seemed to make sense. But then, Lucca had always been very practical. If she caught the earliest possible train she would be home in time to greet Marco as he wakened and to take a breakfast tray up to her sister as a thank-you for her helpfulness.

'Vivien...' Lucca prompted with a tinge of impatience.

'Yes...OK, I'll stay...thank you,' Vivien added stiltedly.

'You must be hungry.'

'No, not at all, 'Vivien declared, for she had no appetite. 'It's been a very long and trying day. Could I go upstairs now?'

Lean, dark face impassive, Lucca gazed back at her with dark-as-midnight eyes as tough as diamonds. 'You surprise me, *cara*. I thought you might view our enforced togetherness as yet another opportunity in your campaign to resurrect our marriage.'

Mortified colour swept away Vivien's pallor. He was making fun of her in the cruellest way. That biting tongue of his had always been the dark side of his keen intelligence. Anger rescued her at what felt like her lowest ebb and her chin came up. 'Perhaps I need to reconsider whether or not you would be worth more effort.'

'In terms of cash…yes,' Lucca countered without hesitation. 'In terms of anything else, we would have to negotiate.'

'I don't know what you're talking about, don't want to know.' Vivien was too worked up to think straight and too exhausted to risk remaining any longer in his vicinity. 'I just want to go to my room.'

'I'll show you up.'

For a self-indulgent instant, she let herself look at Lucca, for she knew she would probably not see him again before she left. Greedily making the most of her chance, she stared and wondered what it was about him that made him so irresistible. His sleek dark good looks, the very masculine beauty of his long, powerful build and that dazzling sex appeal that could shock like a sudden blaze? Or the even more charismatic appeal of his cool, analytical intelligence and that innate reserve that had always shut her out? He had taught her that even with the supposed security of a wedding ring on her finger loving another human being could be agonising.

At the top of the handsome staircase, she paused. 'You're very clever at most things but you actually weren't very good at being married,' she remarked absently half under her breath.

Disconcerted dark golden eyes locked to her with perceptible force. 'Say that again…'

'Marriage was the one thing you hadn't tried and I was a novelty.' Vivien stared at a beautiful inlaid cabinet because she was afraid that if she looked at the dark beauty of him she would lose her nerve. 'You once spent two million pounds on a painting and, after it had hung one night in your apartment, you loaned it out to a museum and I don't think you ever went near it again. The thrill was in the acquisition.'

His sculpted jaw line hardened as he switched on the lamps in the large bedroom he had entered and stood back to allow her to pass. 'You're talking rubbish.'

'No, I was like that painting. Once you got me, you lost interest,' she completed gruffly.

'I don't propose to distinguish your imaginative comments with a response. Use the phone if you require anything.' Lithe as a jungle predator, Lucca strolled back to the door, all male, arrogant and oh, so sure of himself and challenging her at every step. *'Dormi bene.'*

Sleep well? Was he joking? A hysterical laugh was stuck in Vivien's throat and she was trembling all over...

CHAPTER FOUR

REFUSING to surrender to her emotional state, Vivien lifted the phone by the bed to call Bernice. When there was no response at her home, her concern quickened and she rang her sister's mobile phone instead. It took some time before it was answered.

'Vivien?' Bernice's voice was muffled and hard to hear against the music playing in the background. 'Why are you calling? Are you trying to check up on me?'

Vivien marvelled that such loud music did not get on her sister's nerves and understood why her sibling would have been unlikely to hear the phone ringing out in the hall. 'Of course not. But I was a little worried. Apparently, Fabian came to the house earlier when you were out.'

A sharp little silence fell and then Bernice snapped, 'I wasn't out. But when I saw it was him, I couldn't be bothered answering the door. He's such a bore.'

'I'm going to be a bore too and ask you to turn down your music just a tiny bit...if Marco cries, you wouldn't be able to hear him,' Vivien pointed out in a tone of anxious apology. 'Look, I can stay the night in London and return home first thing in the morning, but if you'd prefer me to come back tonight, I will—'

'Oh, don't be stupid. There's no need for you to come rushing back home,' her sister declared impatiently. There was the sound of a door closing and suddenly blessed peace stretched at the other end of the line. 'Marco's fine…sleeping like a log. How did it go with Lucca?'

Legs feeling hollow and weak, Vivien collapsed down on the side of the bed. 'Badly…he's seeing Bliss Masterson, the model, and I met her. She's absolutely gorgeous—'

Bernice giggled like a drain. 'Oh, dear, it's really not been your day! I did warn you, didn't I?'

'Yes, you did…' Vivien conceded thickly.

'Lucca's a complete bastard,' her sibling opined with real venom. 'Did you ask him about the money?'

Vivien swallowed hard. 'Yes…I think that'll be all right.'

'Brilliant!' Bernice exclaimed.

Vivien thought she heard another voice sounding at her sister's end of the line and asked, 'Have you got friends over?'

'Why are you asking me that?' Bernice demanded truculently.

'I thought I heard someone speaking to you—'

'You didn't…it must've been the television. See you tomorrow!'

The line went dead.

Slowly, Vivien replaced the phone.

Lucca was never likely to be part of her life again. A pain that went as sharp and deep as a spear wound pierced her and she quivered. It was more than three years since she had run out of that party at Serafina's apartment after seeing Lucca with yet another highly fanciable female wrapped round him. He had followed her out into the street.

'So you *do* want me the way I want you,' he pronounced with raw satisfaction. 'Don't worry about my companion. She's just window dressing—'

'Does *she* know that?' Vivien was appalled by his attitude.

Lucca shrugged a broad shoulder. 'It's you I want, *bella mia*. Other women can only be substitutes. If you want to blame anyone for that, blame yourself.'

'Don't try to make me responsible for the fact that you're a womaniser!'

'I'm single…I tell no lies and I'm not breaking any rules. Don't be such a prude. If I was as wholesome as you think you'd like me to be, I'd be a married man with children by now and you'd be tormented by the fact that I was morally out of reach. As it is, I'm available and all you need is the courage to stop running away like a little girl from what you know is between us.'

At three in the morning, he came round to her flat and, worn down by stress and longing and relief that he was not after all spending the night in the other woman's arms, she let him in. He pulled her to him in the dim hallway and murmured intently, 'I'll be different with you, *cara*. You will have my exclusive attention—'

'Gosh…' she framed shakily, thinking that he was offering as an extra what she had assumed she could already take for granted.

'And I will make you happy. It can be that easy, that simple,' Lucca whispered with black-velvet cool. 'Why make it difficult?'

But the only thing she found easy was loving him and loving Lucca was not something that she felt she got a choice about. They saw each other whenever they could but there was never enough time to satisfy either of them. Head over heels in love, she did not have a single doubt about their relationship. Within

two months, he asked her to marry him, but the minute
the engagement ring went on her finger the privacy
they had once enjoyed was at an end.

His friends flattered her within his hearing and made
cutting comments behind his back. Lucca, with his
social pedigree and immense wealth, was seen as a
great marital prize and most of the women in his exclusive social circle were downright insulted by his
choice of an unfashionable academic as a bride.
Continual embarrassing and hurtful allusions to his
volatile reputation with her sex, his fabled libido and
her own lack of sophisticated sparkle damaged her
self-esteem and her faith in Lucca even before the
wedding.

At the time, however, she had no awareness of that
reality. The day she married Lucca had been the hap-
piest of her life and their brief honeymoon had been
sheer bliss. Yet, just ten short months later, she had
been desperately lonely and unhappy. Had it not been
for Jasmine Bailey's allegations, though, she would
have remained with Lucca. He had never understood
exactly *why* she had left him, Vivien conceded wretchedly. His apparent infidelity had convinced her that her
agreeing to a divorce was the wisest and kindest option
she could give to a guy who had made it bitterly obvious for weeks beforehand that he very much regretted having married her in the first place…

Disgusted to find tears trickling down her cheeks,
Vivien plunged upright and blundered into the *en suite*
bathroom. Splashing her face, she decided that, since
she was unlikely to fall asleep naturally at nine in the
evening, she would go for a warm bath and hope it
helped her to relax.

Sinking into the fragrant depths of the warm water

a few minutes later, she found herself wondering quite why Bernice disliked Lucca so much. Her sister had never had a good word to say about him and, truth to tell, Lucca had always been a little cool with Bernice. Probably a personality clash. Vivien swallowed painfully and wished she had Marco to cuddle.

A light knock sounded on the bathroom door and she froze in dismay and then sat upright, water sloshing noisily round her as she hugged her knees in an instinctive need to shield her nakedness. 'I'm not dressed!' she yelped in warning to whoever was in the bedroom beyond.

'It's not a problem,' Lucca told her, his dark honeyed drawl roughening the syllables. 'I sent a meal up to you on a tray but you didn't answer the door when it was brought so I said that I would take care of it.'

'I'm not hungry…' she mumbled.

Dark eyes narrowed to gold glittering intensity, Lucca surveyed her. As he'd walked through the door, he had been treated to a tantalising glimpse of delicate white breasts crowned with succulent pink peaks. Hunger hotter than a bonfire held him taut. There she was clutching her knees and, as always, shorn of every artifice. Yet she radiated megawatt appeal. Her baby-fine hair was tousled, damp would-be curls forming above enormous green eyes and a lush mouth as sexy as sin.

'I *am*,' he said almost fiercely.

'Oh, you have the tray, then,' Vivien urged jerkily, fighting to drag her mesmerised eyes from his and failing. He had incredibly beautiful eyes that were bronze in some lights and flamed gold in others. And when he looked at her, a melting sensation formed in her pelvis and thinking rationally became too much of a challenge. He had shed his jacket and tie, undone the collar of his black shirt. He looked dark and dangerous and lethally attractive and little quivers of helpless feminine appreciation were shooting along her nerve-endings.

His sculpted mouth quirked. 'Why aren't you telling me to get out?'

She knew why but was too gutless to tell him. Her mind had already filled with fantasy images in which he would pluck her out of the water, carry her off to bed and sate the uncontrollable craving that he had always unleashed in her.

Lucca tipped his handsome dark head back. In her unshielded and hopeful gaze he had read the answer he had already divined from her silence. In time-honoured style, it was once again his cue to take sexual charge so that she did not have to feel responsible about what she was doing. Lucca was surprised to discover that on this occasion he wanted a greater input from her. Why not? Why should he make it all so easy for her? After all, he had already engineered the entire situation to lead to just such a denouement. Having deliberately dissuaded her from going home to be with the nerd, he had had every intention of seducing her back into his bed for the night. But he was now stubbornly determined that she make her own choice and act accordingly...

'If you want to share my bed tonight, I'll be in the room next door and you can come to me.' Lucca surveyed her dismayed face with grim amusement.

Shocked embarrassment made her fine skin flush red and her mouth had dropped open in disconcertion. 'How...how the heck can you say such a thing to me?'

'Life's short. I'm trying to save us both from growing old and grey while we wait for you to make a decision and act. Either you want me enough to take a risk, or you don't, *cara*,' Lucca delivered silkily. 'The decision is yours.'

Feeling horribly mortified, Vivien listened to the door close on his exit from the adjoining bedroom. He had gone. Blinking in confusion, she stood up in the bath and hauled a towel round her streaming body. She was shaking. He knew her so well. He had recognised her shameless eagerness, realised that she was sitting there in the bath just waiting for him to reach for her. And instead of just doing what he had always done before, instead of doing what came entirely naturally to a male of his dominant temperament, he had derided her passivity and thrown down the gauntlet.

She had never been much good at taking risks. For that reason, everything she had already done that day felt very unreal because she had gone out on a limb to approach Lucca, not just once, but twice. And where had her newly discovered sense of daring got her? It had ripped the lid off all the pathetic little lies she had been telling herself for two years. It had forced her to face just how miserable she really was without Lucca. It was also now persuading her to consider a path to reclaiming her marriage that she had not previously considered.

In spite of Bliss Masterson's wondrous beauty and perfection, Lucca was still attracted to his wife. Instead of being priggish about his blunt way of expressing that news, should she not be grateful for the fact that she could still interest him in that department? After all, if Lucca had found her unattractive there would be no hope whatsoever of achieving a reconciliation. So did that mean she just fell back into his bed?

Wasn't it much too soon for that? Lucca did not suffer from her inhibitions, she reminded herself ruefully. He had a very high sex drive. They *were* still married and it was her fault they had broken up. She had devoted her entire day to telling him that she wanted him back. She could hardly complain that he had put the most literal interpretation on her request. And when Lucca challenged her to take a risk on him wasn't he giving her the hope that they could have a future again?

This was not the time, she told herself urgently, to brood about the reality that she was not the sexy siren type. This could well be her one and only chance to save their marriage and she could not afford to surrender to her own shyness. Having put back on her bra and panties, she hesitated. It would look a little foolish if she got fully dressed just to go next door. After a lot of anxious thought, she yanked the silky tasselled throw off the foot of the bed and anchored it round her like a beach towel.

Before her nerves could seize up, she left the bedroom to blunder through the door of the next room only to find that…it was in darkness and empty and she appeared to be in the wrong place. He wasn't in the room across the corridor either. Hunt the husband, Vivien thought hysterically. Could he have changed his mind?

'No need to sack the house from top to bottom, I'm in here…' Lucca drawled sardonically from somewhere behind her.

Taken by surprise, Vivien whirled round. Her toes caught in the trailing fringe on the throw and tripped her up. With a startled yelp she fell her length in the corridor and knocked the breath from her lungs.

'*Dio mio*… Are you all right?' Lucca leant down to close his hand over one of hers and haul her upright again.

'Absolutely fine!' Vivien gasped, writhing with discomfiture and almost in tears of frustration. It was a challenge to be bold in an area where she had never been confident. And, forced to dress in the equivalent of a sofa cover and flailing around his feet like an idiot, she felt she had hit a new lowest ebb.

For the sake of efficiency, Lucca scooped her up and carried her back into his room, where he settled her carefully down on an area of floor where there were no obstructions.

'So what now?' she framed, hovering like a school-girl.

'I unwrap you before you break a leg.' Closing long fingers into one corner of the throw, Lucca spun her deftly round and removed the offending item before she had even quite grasped what he was doing.

'Oh!' Stripped of her main source of concealment, Vivien crossed her arms over herself and got her first proper look at him.

Lucca was clad only in a pair of boxer shorts. A vibrant image of lean, bronzed masculinity, he made her mouth run dry and she found herself staring. Wide brown shoulders lent definition to powerful pectoral muscles roughened with curling tendrils of black hair above a stomach flat as a washboard. Something akin to a flock of butterflies broke loose in her tummy and the high-wire tension keeping her still leapt up another notch.

'It feels…so strange being here with you again,' she confided breathless with nerves.

'I'd call it erotic…' Lucca countered, strolling fluidly closer to anchor a sure hand into the fall of her tumbled fair hair and tip her head up. 'I feel like a sultan with a slave. I feel that anything I want I can have tonight.'

An apprehensive frown dented her smooth pale brow and then she managed an uncertain laugh, for she knew he could only be joking. 'I wouldn't go quite that far...'

'I think you'll go as far as I want you to, *mia bella*.' He tasted her soft, parted lips with slow, burning precision.

It was like watching a flame dance closer to dynamite; her tummy flipped and her body quivered in expectation. He lifted his arrogant dark head again to scan her with gleaming golden eyes and then he kissed her again with a hot violence of demand that left her clinging to his shoulders to stay upright.

He drew her hands down and removed her bra. Ignoring her startled indrawn breath, he caught her fingers in his before she could turn away in an instinctive need to conceal her nakedness. Appreciative golden eyes lingered on the small pouting swells adorned by coral-pink tips.

'I've missed your body...' Lucca confided.

Her flush of embarrassment started at her collarbone. Pleased though she was by the sentiment, she felt naked and exposed and far too much the focus of attention.

'I shall enjoy becoming reacquainted with it,' Lucca declared, letting his thumbs rub over the tender swollen peaks of her breasts and watching her jerk and strangle a responsive gasp in her throat. Bending down, he lifted her up off her feet into his arms.

'W-where are we going with this? I mean…you and me?' Vivien stammered awkwardly.

'My bed…don't ask trick questions,' Lucca advised. 'You're not subtle enough.'

He laid her down onto the vast smooth expanse of the divan. He had told no lies. He had been straight with her, Lucca told himself squarely. If she chose to play the eternal optimist and reach other assumptions, it was not his problem. He wanted her and she was willing. Why make it any more complicated than that? The low light gilded the silky tumble of her fair hair, accentuating the pale delicacy of her skin and the flawless grace of her slender figure.

He was holding her wrists to the bed to keep her entrapped and a shy smile softened the anxious line of her reddened lips, for the intensity with which he was visually devouring her prone length could only entrance her. There was nothing suspect about the level of his interest. It certainly wasn't a cruel tease. He really, really wanted her. The question of how much he might have wanted Bliss Masterson threatened to intrude and, like someone slamming the door shut on hell, she shut off that thought-train fast.

'You're really beautiful…in your little way,' Lucca completed almost roughly, handsome jaw line squaring as if he was afraid such a compliment might give her ideas above her station.

'That's just what you think,' she dared.

'Doesn't Fabian think the same thing?'

'Fabian?' Her luminous eyes widened in bewilderment, for she could not think how he had become aware even of the existence of the other man, but was not sufficiently concerned by that mystery to enquire into it. 'I shouldn't think he has ever considered my looks. Like me, he's much more interested in practical things—'

'*Dio mio*…what a very sensible attitude,' Lucca murmured between gritted teeth, displeased by the airy manner in which she twinned her own nature to that of another man. 'But then what I think is at this moment…*all* that should count, *bellezza*.'

Her heart clenched at the assurance. 'It does count—'

'So stop trying to edge below the sheet to hide from me. It's been a long time. Let me savour the view,' he urged, directing his attention to the bikini panties she still wore and peeling them off. 'That's better…'

Dark golden eyes flared over her in a sensually assessing arc of confidence and he stepped back to remove his boxer shorts. He was fully aroused and more encouraged than inhibited by an audience. Her face burned hot. She closed her eyes but a wicked tingling had begun low in her belly.

'Look at me…' Lucca ordered thickly as he came down beside her.

Her lashes lifted. He let a knowing fingertip delicately trace the tender thrust of her pink nipples. Her spine arched, arrows of fire shooting to the tight hollow centre of her and she gasped, 'Lucca…'

He bent his dark head and the tip of his tongue stroked the straining tips and her hips shifted against the sheet, intolerable heat beginning to burn the sensitive flesh between her thighs. It had been so long since she was touched and she was shattered by the strength of her own response. She clenched her hands tightly by her sides, striving for control and then losing it just as fast and spearing her fingers into his luxuriant black hair to hold him to her.

He stretched up and pulled her down to him, dipping his tongue in a hungry, sexy forage into the tender interior of her mouth. Again and again he penetrated between her lips until she had both arms wound round him tight to trade kiss for kiss. Her heart was hammering so hard she could only breathe in fevered snatches.

He rolled her half under him and discovered the damp liquid heat between her slender thighs.

'You need me, *cara*...' With a husky laugh of male appreciation, he explored the slick, silken depths of her with expert fingers. The pleasure was a torment that made her twist and turn and moan. She was lost in passion, overwhelmed by the frantic hunger of her own body.

'Lucca, *please*...' she heard herself plead and she didn't care. The wanting inside her had reached such a peak she was utterly controlled by it and helpless.

He flipped her back and plunged into her with an earthy groan. Her slight frame jerked in sexual shock from the power of that invasion and the hot glide of his rigid shaft as he penetrated her. He pushed her legs high, ground deeper into her. Her excitement flared to fever pitch. In the midst of that wildness that she had never known with him before, she dimly recognised the difference in him, but the raw, helpless pleasure taking her by storm wiped out every other awareness. Sensation sent her rushing to an explosive peak and the shattering release of joyous abandonment rippled through her in wave after wave of delight.

In the aftermath of that sensual storm, Vivien was weak and in shock. She wrapped her arms tight round Lucca while he was struggling to recapture his breath. She felt incredibly happy. They were together again,

Vivien thought, weak with relief and gratitude for the opportunity. Yes, lots of things still had to be ironed out, but essentially their separation was over and they were at the outset of a new beginning in their marriage.

'Life just wasn't life without you,' she mumbled in the grip of her emotions and trying very hard not to get weepy, but it was difficult because she was on a high.

'Is that a fact, *cara*?' Lucca stretched with the slumberous grace of a panther and dropped a kiss to her brow.

He tried not to laugh at the way she was clutching him while secretly enjoying the power of being so indispensable. For just those few seconds it was as if he were inhabiting a time slip and then crash, bang the curtain whipped up again on his recollection of the past two years and the cold and the steel and the darkness entered back into his soul. He gazed down at her, brooding dark golden eyes semi-concealed by lush black lashes.

She spread appreciative fingers across the hard contours of bone and sinew that lay below the smooth bronzed skin of his shoulders and stared up at his lean, darkly handsome face. She breathed in deep. 'I…I still love you.'

'I'm honoured.' Lucca lifted a hand and indicated a tiny space. 'Do you love me this much? Or this much…?' He stretched lean brown fingers wider apart.

Her shy smile crept across her reddened mouth for she believed he was teasing her. 'Oh, at least *two* hand spans…'

'But I didn't ask for love…I only wanted sex.'

Eyes veiling, Vivien went pink and winced. 'I wish you wouldn't talk like that.'

'If you love me enough, you'll forgive me,' Lucca declared with sardonic bite.

Vivien stilled, only then recognising the jarring note in his dark deep accented drawl and grasping that something was wrong. He rolled her off him and sprang out of bed. He was all sleek power and strong muscles, a virile male in the very peak of condition. She stared, a hollow feeling in the pit of her tummy. It was as though he had cut her in two. She had given herself in trust and offered her love and he had taken one and discarded the other. *I only wanted sex.* Was he serious? She trembled, feeling sick with humiliation.

The phone by the bed buzzed loudly. With a muttered imprecation in his own language, Lucca swept up the phone. Suddenly he fell still, his hard jaw line squaring. 'Yes, I am Lucca Saracino. What has happened?'

The gravity of his voice made her push herself up in the bed and stare. His natural colour had leeched from below his olive skin. 'Which hospital? How is he?' he demanded flatly. 'How did this occur?'

While he listened, his lean, powerful face clenched hard and shadowed. 'Thank you,' he breathed gruffly. 'I will get to the hospital as soon as possible.'

Tossing the phone aside, Lucca shot Vivien a chilling look of fierce condemnation. 'That was the police. An hour ago they took Marco to hospital. He has cuts and bruises. He was found on the street on his own.'

Vivien could not credit what he was telling her. 'I beg your pardon…?'

'Your sister tried to reclaim him but was considered

too drunk to be entrusted with his care a second time. Apparently, she took him to a party and he wandered out of the house without anyone even noticing that he was missing!' Lucca framed between clenched teeth.

'Oh, dear heaven, no!' Gripped by fear on her son's behalf, Vivien fought through her welter of horrified disbelief that such an event could have taken place and concentrated on what was important. '*Hospital?* Marco's in hospital? Has he been hurt?'

Scorching golden eyes challenged her. 'How the hell could you leave my infant son in that selfish bitch's care?'

'Please tell me how Marco is…is he all right?' Vivien pressed strickenly.

'*Dannazione!* What do you call "all right"? He has cuts and bruises and he's terrified. He could have been kidnapped, killed, *anything*! I thank God that He was merciful and that we still have a son,' Lucca launched at her in a black seething fury, hauling on clothes as he spoke. 'Someone's going to answer for this outrage!'

CHAPTER FIVE

'Someone's going to answer for this outrage.' That
threat still echoing in her ears, Vivien sat silent and
rigid in the rear of Lucca's limousine. The buck stops
here, she thought wretchedly. She was responsible for
Marco and she had placed him in Bernice's care. Out
in a street without an adult looking out for him, Marco
might so easily have been run over by a car. The son
she adored might have died because she had utilised
poor judgement.

But how could she have guessed that Bernice would
lie to her? Her sister had lied to cover up the fact that
she'd not been at home where she'd been pretending
to be, but actually out socialising in the company of
other people. How could she have known that Bernice
would act in such an irresponsible way? Taking Marco
from his bed to go to a party and then imbibing so
much alcohol that she could not be trusted to watch
over her nephew. Vivien felt sick to the stomach with
guilt and the horror of what might have been. She did
not feel that she could fault Lucca for the ferocious
anger that had darkened his gaze to a hard black onslaught.

'Why didn't you arrange proper care for Marco?'
Lucca enquired coldly.

Desperate to reach her son's side so that she could
soothe his fear and his hurts, Vivien had to struggle
to think straight and answer. 'Blame Jasmine Bailey
and that newspaper article—'

'I'm blaming you,' Lucca slotted in harshly.

Vivien knotted her hands tightly together. 'Rosa, Marco's nanny, only works for me part-time and she doesn't do evenings. I used to have a student who babysat for me occasionally but she's graduated now. This arrangement with Bernice was a last-minute thing. Rosa was to put Marco to bed for her. I didn't expect to be so late coming back...but I've got to be honest,' she muttered tightly. 'I didn't think that I would be taking a risk either. I trusted my sister—'

'*Inferno!* You *trusted* Bernice?' Brilliant black eyes struck merciless sparks off her anxious face. 'She's too spoilt and self-centred to put a child's needs ahead of her own desires. How could you possibly have trusted her?'

'I never thought for one moment that Bernice would do anything that might put Marco in jeopardy,' Vivien countered with driven sincerity. 'Obviously I was wrong and I don't think I'll ever forgive myself for that—'

A sardonic black brow lifted. 'I'll never forgive this,' Lucca stated with chilling cool.

Vivien flinched. She was in total turmoil. It was a torment for her to think of Marco suffering without her comforting presence. It was an agony to deal with her own guilt and the depth of her sibling's betrayal. It was also excruciating to acknowledge that just over an hour ago, Lucca, having made passionate love to her again, had then rejected her and her love in the most painful and humiliating manner.

One minute she had naively believed that they were on the threshold of a new beginning and a few seconds later all her hopes had been brutally destroyed. At that instant there was no part of Vivien that was not feeling mental anguish. Why had she never faced just how cruel Lucca could be? She had always preferred to overlook or excuse the darker side of his strong character. He had never compromised, never conceded his own mistakes and now he denied forgiveness and compassion for human error as well.

'Once I forgave you for a lot more...' Vivien breathed shakily.

His dark as midnight eyes narrowed and challenged. 'I did nothing that required forgiveness.'

It was the proverbial last straw and all that was required to break the last strand of her tenuous control. Her fine bone structure was tautly delineated by the strain etched in her delicate features but her green eyes were bright as jewels in their angry conviction. 'Didn't you? You may love Marco now, but when I fell pregnant you acted like a teenager trapped into a shotgun marriage!'

Lucca was transfixed by that offensive accusation. Taken entirely by surprise, he could not immediately credit that so quiet and peaceful a woman could suddenly turn so belligerent. *'Come—?'*

'Don't you dare deny it!' Vivien snapped at him like a small spitting cat.

Lucca made a fast recovery. 'I've no intention of denying that I was annoyed when you chose to become pregnant regardless of my reservations—'

'I did not *choose* to become pregnant!'

Lucca ignored her interruption. 'We were newly married. I wanted to wait for a few years before we became a family and you were well aware of that fact. When you decided to disregard my wishes—'

'Stop right there!' Vivien was reduced to holding up two dissenting hands. 'You're not listening to me.

I don't believe what I'm hearing either. It never once crossed my mind that you suspected me of having planned my pregnancy…why didn't you tell me that at the time?'

'Oh, you know…' Lucca murmured, smoother than the finest silk. 'I was doing that teenage-boy thing…being mature about the shotgun marriage sensation for the baby's sake!'

Her face flamed with embarrassment. 'You still think you can be smart at my expense. Well, I don't like arguing but I have to speak up in my own defence—'

'The suspense is killing me,' Lucca interposed lethally.

Both her hands knotted into fists. 'Why the heck would you believe that I would deliberately have opted for a pregnancy that you didn't want?'

'I worked long hours and you didn't like it. I suspect that you hoped that the baby would act like a dutiful ball and chain on the domestic front and bring me home more often.' Formidable dark golden eyes assessed her in search of a single sign of betraying guilt. 'You faced me with a *fait accompli*. I was very angry with you but there was nothing I could reasonably do or say. Honour demanded I accept that you were carrying my child and make the best of it.'

'So you worked longer hours than ever, practically stopped speaking to me and decided to conduct business on your yacht to ensure that I saw even less of you,' Vivien cut in tightly, unimpressed. 'Honour did not demand any great acceptance or sacrifice from you!'

The faintest colour now demarcated the fabulous

high cheekbones that lent his dark features such magnetism. 'I disagree—'

'Well, you can disagree all you like!' Vivien launched at him with vehemence. 'But I'm telling you now and I am not lying…I didn't set out to have Marco. I was very shocked when I realised I'd conceived.'

Lucca regarded her without any visible reaction at all.

'For goodness' sake, I'm not the sneaky type,' she pointed out in blunt additional protest. 'I wasn't careless when I was taking the contraceptive pill either. Why didn't you make allowances for the fact that there is a *known* failure rate?'

His strong mouth compressed. 'I don't remember thinking about that.'

'It was my doctor's belief that my pregnancy fell into a small per cent category of risk. But when I tried to discuss that with you, you'd leave the room or start talking on the phone—'

'So I'm a guy…not up for the touchy-feely girlie chats,' Lucca pronounced in cool justification of his blocking tactics.

'You should know by now that I'm not deceitful,' Vivien told him in stressed reproach for what she saw as a most unjust suspicion. 'I conceived because my birth control failed me. I'm shocked that you could have thought anything else.'

By that stage, the limousine was pulling up outside the well-lit exterior of the hospital. It took less than a second for Vivien to forget the argument. She leapt up, wrenched open the passenger door and surged out of the limo on a wave of fevered determination to fill her empty arms with her son.

Lucca steered her in the direction of the reception desk. As they identified themselves an older man approached and introduced himself as a policeman. Blind and apparently deaf to the necessity of the explanations to be made, Vivien began walking away until Lucca closed a restraining hand to her elbow.

They learned that Marco had wandered out of a rear door in the house where the party was being held. A neighbour climbing out of her car had seen Marco and had intercepted him before he could make it out on to the busy road. Having no idea where the child had come from, the woman had contacted the authorities. By the time that Bernice had realised that Marco was missing, the police had arrived. Presented with a distressed child, who had been bleeding from an apparent fall, they had refused to hand him over to Bernice. Instead the police had insisted that Marco be checked out at a hospital and that his mother be contacted. However, when Vivien had failed to answer her mobile phone official channels had been used to track down Lucca's phone number.

Vivien requested the name and address of the kindly neighbour who had rescued Marco earlier that evening. She wanted to write a letter thanking the woman whose timely intervention might well have saved her son from far worse injury. As she moved away, overwhelmingly eager to be reunited with her child, Bernice approached her. 'I bet you're blaming me for this nightmare!'

Although that provocative greeting struck a very wrong note in the circumstances, Vivien did note that her sister's eyes were swollen and distraught. Her compassionate heart softened. She knew that Bernice had already had to endure a stern warning from the police for her carelessness and for the amount of alcohol she had taken while she was supposed to be looking after a young child. 'I just wish you hadn't lied to me about where you were when I phoned you earlier—'

'I was certain you'd make a big fuss if you knew I'd gone out. It was only a little white lie. If everything hadn't all gone wrong, you'd never have found out. I didn't think there could be any harm in my taking Marco out with me!' Bernice instantly began to argue in her own defence. 'He was perfectly happy. I put him in a cot in my friend's house and he was fine. How was I to know he would climb out of the cot?'

'If only you had told me when I phoned that you needed me to come back immediately, so that you could go out.' Vivien sighed. 'I'm not blaming you—'

'But I *am* blaming you, Bernice,' Lucca slotted in with chilling coldness, banding an arm to Vivien's taut spine. 'Nor will we discuss this further. Right now, Marco's need for us is of greater importance.'

'I'll be staying with friends tonight,' Bernice snapped with a defiant toss of her head and she stalked off in a temper before her sister could intervene.

Lucca had arranged a private room for Marco's use and it was there that Marco was finally reunited with his parents. Impervious to the efforts of the nurse attempting to comfort him, Marco was hunched in the corner of a metal cot sobbing his heart out. At the sound of his mother's soft voice, he clawed himself upright, huge dark eyes telegraphing hope. His brow was scraped, his nose cut and there was a purplish bruise on the side of one chubby cheek. In tears herself and striving to repress all pointless conjecture about the further evils that might have befallen the child she adored, Vivien scooped his solid little body up and hugged him tightly to her. At that instant she didn't ever want to let go of him again.

Finally raising his curly dark head from his mother's shoulder, Marco stared in wide-eyed astonishment at his tall darkly handsome father. *'Papà...?'* he questioned doubtfully.

For the very first time, Vivien watched her son hold out his arms to Lucca. But no sooner had Marco made that apparent choice between them than he changed his mind again, clung fearfully to his mother and burst back into floods of tears.

'He's not used to seeing us together. It's very confusing for him and he's not in the mood to be upset.' Lucca proffered that opinion half under his breath and his intonation was grim.

Vivien was very pale. The unfamiliar sight of his parents together distressed their child and whose fault was that? It was an issue that cut like a knife to the very heart of her already burdened conscience. She had ended their marriage. She was responsible for the reality that Marco was growing up with a father who could only feature in his life as an occasional visitor. Biting her lip and tasting blood in her dry mouth, she fought back the welling tears and promised herself there and then that, no matter what the personal cost, she would make sure that Lucca had every possible opportunity to make up for that lost time with his son. That was not something that should hinge on Lucca's lack of response to her intensely personal attempt to put their broken marriage back together again, she told herself staunchly. Never again would she allow her anguish and hurt pride to interfere with Lucca's relationship with Marco.

'Let's get him home,' Lucca advised with decisive cool.

Inside the limo, Marco was buckled into a car seat. Still on the breathless edge of a threatening sob, he reached out and closed a small hand tightly into the fabric of Lucca's jacket sleeve. Although it was obvious that their son was fighting sleep, he would not let his eyes close and kept on glancing anxiously at each of his parents in turn as though to reassure himself of their continuing presence.

'He's had a frightening experience. It'll take time for him to recover from his ordeal,' Lucca opined, his tone light for his son's benefit but his brilliant eyes hard as polished steel, for the little boy's normal buoyant, trusting confidence was now strikingly absent.

Weighed down with guilt, Vivien evaded his accusing scrutiny. It was her fault that at the tender age of eighteen months Marco had learnt that his safe little world could turn scary and threatening and that his mother was not always there when he needed her.

Lucca was not impressed by his first glimpse of Vivien's minute rose-covered cottage. He banged his head on a low-slung beam just inside the door and was in the act of suppressing a succinct swear word when a tiny set of needle-sharp teeth nipped into his trouser leg. Assaulted by a small, wildly barking mop of wiry black hair, he stepped back out of reach.

The dog lurched, fell over and played dead.

'Oh, my goodness, you shouldn't have moved so quickly!' Vivien gasped in dismay. 'Jock was depending on you for support.'

'Jock…my Jock…' Marco demonstrated his first sign of returning independence and animation by scrambling out of his mother's arms to pet the dog.

His incredulity growing, Lucca watched while Vivien and his son fussed over an animal that, in his opinion, was staging an award-winning performance.

'He bit me,' Lucca breathed drily.

'Oh, my goodness, I can't believe that he would do anything like that. But if he did, you must've given him an awful fright!' Vivien lamented, engaged in searching the still mop of black hair for vital signs of life. 'Jock's very sensitive.'

Jock twitched, snuffled and opened bright, beady eyes.

'*Dio mio*...is that a fact?' Lucca breathed, reluctantly enthralled by the graceful dramatic touches at which the little animal excelled.

'He had such a traumatic time of it before he came to us,' Vivien told him earnestly while she carefully raised the little terrier upright again on his three sturdy legs. 'Someone abandoned him out on the road. While he was chasing cars trying to find his owner again he got hurt. He's a little suspicious of men but he's a wonderful watchdog and quite devoted to Marco.'

Jock contrived to look simultaneously tragic and a master of one-upmanship. Having walked the first round in the popularity contest, he trotted past Lucca with his tail held high. Vivien carried Marco upstairs and Lucca followed. He was seriously underwhelmed by his surroundings. It was a shabby, chic dwelling designed for very small people who did not suffer from claustrophobia. To watch Marco being tucked into the cot beside Vivien's bed, Lucca had to stand out on the landing. His extravagantly handsome face was by then clenched in tough, uncompromising lines. He was sincerely angry that Marco was being denied the space, luxury and toys that he considered to be his son's most basic right and due.

Vivien watched Marco tense and raise his curly head in dismay when his father shifted position beyond the doorway. 'He's scared you're going to leave. I think he feels safer with both of us here.'

'I'll stay until he's asleep,' Lucca declared.

The toddler focused huge, sleepy eyes on his father. Vivien averted her attention again. It felt so strange to see father and son interact. For the first time she was seeing the extra dimension to Marco's world, the dimension where only Lucca held sway. Her son was intensely attached to Lucca, much more attached than she had ever dreamt he could be. Why had she naively assumed that as Marco's mother she would automatically command the lion's share of her son's affection? Even as she watched Marco stretched out a small, hopeful hand through the bars of the cot and Lucca finally strode into the room with a rueful laugh of acceptance.

Sinking down on the edge of her bed, Lucca leant forward and clasped his son's seeking fingers. Marco smiled happily and finally closed his eyes. Vivien could quite easily have burst into tears at that point. She was seeing stuff she had never thought she would see: Lucca being tender and protective, Marco revealing his total trust and sense of security in his father's presence. The minutes passed in silence. The lamplight gleamed over Lucca's luxuriant cropped black hair, picking up on the dense length of long spiky lashes as dark as charcoal. At length, he settled Marco's relaxed hand down on the mattress with infinite gentleness. Watching them together, her throat tightened.

'Let's go downstairs,' Lucca murmured quietly. 'It's late but I have a couple of things I want to say.'

In the sitting room, Vivien closed her hands together in a nervous gesture and then hurriedly folded her arms. 'I know you're blaming me for everything and you're right. What took place tonight was entirely my fault.'

'I appreciate the way you so frequently save me from the necessity of criticising you,' Lucca drawled. 'You rush with suicidal eagerness to put your head in the noose.'

A flush of discomfiture washed her delicate face but her chin tilted. 'I believe in taking responsibility for my mistakes.'

Brilliant dark golden eyes met hers with level cool and command. 'That's commendable and very apt for the occasion because what I'm about to say is likely to prove challenging for you.'

He looked utterly unapproachable. Yet it was only a few hours since he had been in bed with her. The ill-timed intimacy of that recollection made her fair skin burn and sparked enough mental turmoil to make her strained gaze duck away from his. If the detachment he exuded had been measurable in terms of actual distance he would have been a thousand miles away.

'I want you to move back to London.'

Vivien froze. The tense silence seemed to surge like a rushing wave breaking with almost deafening force against her eardrums.

'I want the chance to be a real father to my son,' Lucca imparted with a measured clarity of tone that telegraphed his desire to make every word hit the right target. 'But I can't achieve that with an extensive ge-

ographical divide between us. I'd like to see Marco
whenever I choose and a lot more often. My time with
him shouldn't always feel like a special occasion. I
need the option of sharing the ordinary days too. I'd
prefer to leave the lawyers out of it as well. I think
that you and I will deal better on a more informal and
friendly basis.'

Taken aback, Vivien strained to comprehend his ex-
act meaning. Was he asking her to move back in with
him? No, no, don't go there, her brain urged her in
disgust at the weakness betrayed by her own eager
wish for such an approach from him. No, of course
Lucca wasn't suggesting reconciliation. He was talking solely about Marco and his desire to normalise his
relationship with his child. But when he talked of leaving his lawyers out of the equation and mentioned as-
piring to a more informal and friendly arrangement
with her, sheer surprise at that unexpected develop-
ment threw her into a loop.

'Yes…er…but moving to London,' she mumbled
uncertainly, playing for time while she endeavoured to
work out what exactly he meant by that invitation.
Friendship? Platonic friendship? What else?

'I'm quite sure some other academic institution
would kill to have you or you could concentrate on
research for a while. I would take care of everything,'
Lucca told her softly as she turned vague troubled eyes
of clear trusting green on him. 'I know how much you
hate upheaval. Obviously you can retain this house
and rent it out. All such matters would be dealt with
on your behalf and according to your wishes. Naturally
I will also cover all your expenses in London—'

'No, that wouldn't be necessary—'

'But I would insist. I'm not in a position to relocate.

You should not suffer in any way from a move that will benefit me. In any case...' keen dark eyes rested on her perturbed expression '...now that we understand each other better, I'm sure I can speak with less fear of injuring my access to my son.'

Vivien lost colour at that veiled gibe. 'You can say anything you like,' she hastened to assure him while wondering dimly where he got the idea that she understood him better when she had never understood him in the slightest.

'I consider this house or even its London equivalent to be an unacceptable home for my son.'

Her bemused gaze widened. 'But what's wrong with this house?'

'I object to Marco being raised in a hovel.'

She flushed. 'For goodness' sake, this is hardly a hovel!'

'It is on my terms. To bring Marco up in such a home is to cruelly deny everything that he is. He is a Saracino,' Lucca asserted with cool pride. 'He has a proud family name and lineage and even at this age he should be able to enjoy all the benefits of Saracino achievements.'

A *hovel*? Vivien swallowed hard. She had almost snapped back a defiant answer but she was badly hampered by the kind of mind that always examined both sides of an equation. It was true that Marco was the son of a very rich man and that measured against Lucca's vast wealth her home could only seem poor. Was that fair to Marco? she was being forced to ask herself for the first time. Should she have allowed her personal preference for independence to rule the lifestyle choices she had made? Had she been horribly selfish when she'd denied her son the trappings of luxury? Whatever, she was learning that Lucca had very much resented her decision to raise his only child outside the privileged world that was his own.

'You're certainly giving me a lot to think about,' she muttered heavily.

'I hope so. My estrangement from my son has been a cause of great bitterness to me,' Lucca admitted without hesitation. 'I have been excluded from his life on almost all fronts and now I want all that to change. Are you willing to rise to that challenge?'

Her head was buzzing with the bewildering surge of semi-formed thoughts produced by stress and exhaustion. She drew in a shaky breath. 'I need to think about this.'

'Unfortunately, I'm not in the mood to be patient. You dislike being hurried into decisions but I feel I have the right to be selfish and put Marco's needs first.'

'Putting Marco's needs first could never be judged selfish,' Vivien hurried to assure him.

'If you truly believe what you are saying, then you give Marco the chance to enjoy the comfort of easy access to *both* his parents,' Lucca countered levelly.

Vivien was very tense, for the discussion was moving far too fast for her liking and she felt cornered. 'If only it were that simple...'

'But it *is*. Sit back, smell the roses. Let other people deal with the hassle on your behalf, *cara*.'

His incredibly sexy drawl vibrated through her tense frame and she struggled not to respond to it. When Lucca spoke in that darkly sensual, soothing tone, she felt dizzy and the very personification of weak womanhood. Only the powerful pain of the recent past held her back from the brink of a foolish decision. She loved him but he did not love her. Furthermore it was very possible that he had had sex with her purely as a means of expressing his contempt. So dark, so dreadful was that suspicion that she immediately shied away from it and felt quite ill. But her awareness that Lucca could be frighteningly hard, cruel and unforgiving lingered like a steadying influence on her softer nature.

She had ended their marriage. She was responsible for the damaging limitations that had restricted Lucca's ability to build up a relationship with his son. But in an effort to redress that wrong was she prepared to give up everything that she had worked so hard to build up over the past two years? She worked in a specialist field of botany and options for career moves were few and far between. It could well be a long time before she found an equally suitable position. On the other hand the opportunity and excuse to spend more time with Marco before he outgrew his baby years would be very welcome to her.

'There has to be an alternative,' Vivien mused unevenly, telling herself that it would be most unwise for her to aspire to any friendlier or less formal relationship with Lucca. Unhappily a certain amount of distance was going to be the only way she could handle any further exposure to Lucca. Anything else would break her heart all over again. And her heart was already cracked right down the middle.

What else could it be? Sudden seething emotional pain gripped her. *I only wanted sex,* he had told her bluntly. Yet sex, and surely far more exciting sex than she could supply, was easily available to him. How far could contempt drive a guy like Lucca? There he was, megawatt handsome and confident, and he had the most beautiful woman in the world in his life. But

in spite of those exciting realities, Lucca had chosen
instead to bed his wife again. What did that tell her?
And what had Lucca himself said? He had asked her
the cruellest question, she recalled, sinking deeper into
the hold of her despairing thoughts. Do you love me
this much? Or this much?

'There is no alternative,' Lucca delivered grimly,
studying the purity of her pensive profile with bleak
condemnation. Anger lay like a cold weight of ice inside him. Her physical delicacy and her aura of vul-
nerability seemed the very essence of sweet old-
fashioned femininity. But she had been cold as charity
when she'd walked out on him. In addition, he was
not going to beg for time with the son she had virtually
stolen from him. Either she gave ground, and a lot of
it, or he would fight and he would fight dirty without
a shred of conscience.

Vivien wasn't listening. At that instant, she was ac-
knowledging with great sadness and shame that,
whether she liked it or not, Lucca had had good reason
to scorn her renewed declaration of love and question
the level of her commitment to any such promise. Two
years ago, she had, after all, let him down very badly
on that score. Her once fervent avowals of love must
have seemed like lies to him after she had left him,
deaf to his plea of innocence and convinced of his
infidelity. She, who prided herself on her loyalty and
dependability, had displayed feet of solid clay.

'If you choose not to facilitate my need to get to
know my son better, I will take this to court.'

The cold, precise edge to his accented drawl cut
through her abstraction like a scythe. Her head spun
round, jewelled green eyes full of dismay. 'Court? Are
you serious?'

Lucca gazed steadily back at her, the uncompromising force of his dark, intense eyes making her tummy take a nervous flip. 'Where Marco is concerned, I've been out in the cold long enough. You seem to take for granted the belief that Marco should live with you rather than with me.'

'I don't...I really don't!' Vivien had turned very pale because she was shaken by his perceptiveness. It was true that she had never even considered the idea that the child she adored might reside with anyone other than her.

Lucca recognised her denial as a lie and her complacency outraged his sense of justice. 'I no longer have Jasmine Bailey's sordid allegations hanging over my head. Why do you find it so difficult to think of me as a parent with a potential right to custody of my own child? How do you think I felt tonight when I heard Marco had been out on the street on his own? Lost and hurt and scared? Dependent on the compassion of a stranger?'

'I imagine you felt as absolutely dreadful about it as I did,' Vivien breathed unsteadily, folding her arms as if to ward off that attack.

'You're wrong. I was furious with *you*. You entrusted the most precious being in my life to Bernice the party girl!' Scorching golden eyes assailed her in angry judgement of that mistake. 'Marco could have died and I am quite prepared to take tonight's events into a court room and let a judge decide who most deserves care and control of a vulnerable child!'

White as milk, Vivien clasped her trembling hands tight in on themselves. Her green eyes were dark with stress and fear. 'There's no need to threaten me with that course—'

'*Dannazione!* There is every need. My son was born eighteen months ago and right from the start it was clear that I was to be granted only the most minor role in his life,' Lucca bit out harshly. 'My child was two days old before I even knew he had been born! Have you any idea how that made me feel? Time and time again my perfectly reasonable requests to see my child were rescheduled and often for the meanest of excuses! One tiny sniffle and you wouldn't let him out of your sight!'

His accusations, she registered in a sudden awful moment of insight into her own behaviour, had a horrible edge of truth. She had always loathed the Saturdays when she had had to hand her baby over to the nanny, who, acting as go-between, took him off to spend a few hours with Lucca. Initially Marco had cried pitifully at being divided from his mother and, although that had passed, Vivien had still hated the pain of having to part with him in the first place. She had felt as though Marco were being cruelly snatched from her and had worried herself sick while he'd been away from her for she had had the greatest difficulty in picturing Lucca the womaniser as a caring father.

In point of fact, she had resented the legal requirement to share her son with the same male who she believed had betrayed her by taking another woman into his bed. She was shocked by that belated realisation that, without ever appreciating what she was doing, she had been trying to punish Lucca by restricting access to Marco. Steeped in genuine regret, Vivien stared back at Lucca with hollowed miserable eyes. 'I'm so sorry...'

His stunning dark golden gaze challenged hers.

Play the
Lucky Hearts
Game

and get...

2 FREE BOOKS
and a **FREE MYSTERY GIFT...**

YOURS to KEEP!

yes! I have scratched off the silver card.
Please send me my *2 FREE BOOKS* and
FREE mystery GIFT. I understand that I am
under no obligation to purchase any books as
explained on the back of this card.

Scratch Here!
then look below to see
what your cards get you...
2 Free Books & a Free
Mystery Gift!

306 HDL D34X

106 HDL D35H

FIRST NAME   LAST NAME

ADDRESS

APT.#   CITY

STATE/PROV.   ZIP/POSTAL CODE

(H-P-11/04)

Twenty-one gets you
2 FREE BOOKS
and a *FREE MYSTERY GIFT!*

Twenty gets you
2 FREE BOOKS!

Nineteen gets you
1 FREE BOOK!

TRY AGAIN!

Offer limited to one per household and not valid to current Harlequin Presents® subscribers.
All orders subject to approval.

The Harlequin Reader Service® — Here's how it works:

If offer card is missing write to: Harlequin Reader Service, 3010 Walden Ave., P.O. Box 1867, Buffalo NY 14240-1867

BUSINESS REPLY MAIL
FIRST-CLASS MAIL   PERMIT NO. 717-003   BUFFALO, NY

POSTAGE WILL BE PAID BY ADDRESSEE

HARLEQUIN READER SERVICE
3010 WALDEN AVE
PO BOX 1867
BUFFALO NY 14240-9952

NO POSTAGE
NECESSARY
IF MAILED
IN THE
UNITED STATES

'Then don't waste my time now and don't force me to take you to court to fight for Marco.'

That blunt warning shook Vivien. He was serious. He was willing to fight for custody of Marco and possibly even eager for the excuse to do so. Furthermore, she only had herself to blame for the depth of his sense of injustice for she had not been generous with the amount of time she had allowed him to spend with his son.

'Obviously, I don't want that either,' she muttered tautly. 'I'm willing to make compromises. Exactly what do you want from me?'

A chilling smile of triumph slashed Lucca's cool, sensual mouth. His lean, hard-boned face was stunningly handsome but strikingly hard and unyielding. 'Reparation.'

CHAPTER SIX

AROUND a day and a half later, Vivien tidied her hair in her bedroom. The once-cluttered room was a good deal emptier than it had been the day before when a removal firm had arrived to pack the clothes, toys, books and nursery goods she would be taking with her. Lucca's promise of furnished accommodation had been welcome because Bernice was remaining in the house.

Reparation, Lucca had called the debt he said she owed him. She had been appalled by his threat to challenge her custody of Marco and in that same instant her choice had been made. When Lucca had made it clear that he was even prepared to use Marco's ordeal in the street to represent her as being an unfit parent, she had been utterly devastated.

There never had been any middle ground with Lucca, she acknowledged unhappily. Either one was with him or one was against him. It did not take great imagination to guess where a soon-to-be ex-wife who had sinned against him figured on that scale. Yet to those he cared about Lucca was the very truest of friends, who would offer every possible support in adversity without any expectation of return. But Lucca also made a very cold and implacable enemy. Once she had held special status in his world but not any more, she conceded dully, painfully aware of what she had stupidly surrendered of her own accord.

She had no idea how his justifiable annoyance at

seeing so little of Marco had translated into the passionate sexual encounter that he had allowed to take place between them. She found it impossible to believe that Lucca could have found her too tempting to resist. She was no Helen of Troy and scarcely so beautiful that she could deprive any mortal man of his wits. Of course, Lucca never had been either easily understood or predictable. Humiliatingly, he had calmly dismissed what they had shared as just sex. Was that the truth? Or simply what he preferred to believe? Wasn't it still possible that that passion could spark again into something that might be built on firmer foundations? Even a new beginning?

With a guilty little quiver at her reluctance to let go of her own most precious dream, Vivien shut down that dangerous high-risk thought train. Ostensibly, she was moving to London at Lucca's request solely for his benefit and her son's. Conscience told her that she did owe Lucca some compensation for the effect the breakdown of their marriage had had on his relationship with Marco. But at the same time she was also clinging fast to those promising words, 'friendly and informal'. Lucca was about to become part of her life again. She would see him, get the chance to talk to him and maybe the differences that lay between them could be slowly dissolved.

From such small and humble beginnings, acorns had grown into giant oaks, and, when it came to Lucca Saracino, she loved him enough to take the rough with the smooth and be patient. All she longed for was just one more chance at getting it right with him. She would do absolutely anything to get that chance. Her eyes stung with embarrassing tears and she blinked them back. Mortified by her own desperate fervour, she laid down the hairbrush and hurried downstairs. A car was coming to collect her and Marco.

Bernice strolled out of the kitchen with a glass of wine. 'So you're still going ahead with this?'

Beneath her sibling's censorious appraisal, Vivien tensed. 'Yes.'

'I just can't believe that you can let him make such a fool of you again.' The tall brunette dealt Vivien a speaking look of disgust. 'Lucca Saracino just jerks your strings like a puppet master and you do exactly what he wants!'

'It's really not like that.' Vivien sighed, touched by what she deemed to be her sister's partisan sympathies but wishing that the other woman would calm down enough to try and understand her point of view. 'Lucca wants to see more of Marco and he deserves that chance. Lucca and Marco are really close. Seeing them together made me appreciate that Lucca is just as important to Marco as I am.'

Full raspberry-tinted mouth set in a scornful slant of disbelief, Bernice mimicked playing a violin. 'So, you've resigned from your job and you're moving back to London solely for the most pure of altruistic reasons?'

Her fair skin taking on a guilty pink hue, Vivien bent down to fuss with Jock's carrier box. Behind the gated door, the little terrier was staging a massive sulk. 'Maybe I'm just trying to make up for some of the mistakes I've made.'

'Why can't you admit the truth? You've still got the hots for Lucca and you're being so accommodating because you're hoping like hell that he'll take you back!'

'Well, if I am,' Vivien said a little gruffly, 'it would be my problem, not yours.'

Taken aback by that unexpectedly defiant response, Bernice gasped. 'Don't you have any shame? Any pride?'

Vivien considered those questions. Shame and pride had influenced the speed with which she had abandoned her marriage two years earlier. She had listened to Bernice's tough talk then and perhaps she had listened rather too well. She had been terrified that if she hung around she would end up forgiving Lucca's extra-marital activities. Horribly conscious of her own essential weakness where Lucca was concerned, Vivien had then got tough with herself. But this time around she was dealing with the reality that she was not the wholly innocent victim she had once believed herself to be. She had made a couple of huge errors with Lucca. He might not have been perfect husband material, but when he *had* been with her she had been incredibly happy. Admittedly, he hadn't been with her very often. However, life without him had been deeply hollow and miserable.

'That smug bastard you married must be loving every minute of this!' Bernice slung at her with disdain.

Vivien looked up again with a reproachful frown. 'Why do you dislike Lucca so much?'

Twin spots of red fired over her sibling's cheekbones. She tossed her head, glossy long dark hair tumbling round her shoulders. 'I just don't like the way he treats you…you *know* that.'

But Vivien still felt bewildered by the pure depth of her sister's animosity. 'But why are you so vicious about him?'

A rare look of discomfiture clouded Bernice's lovely face and then her sultry mouth twisted. 'Possibly I know a thing or two about Lucca that would shock you!'

Silence fell, a sudden sharp silence laden with Vivien's dismay and concern. 'What do you mean?'

The bell went: the limo had arrived.

But Vivien was still staring at her sister. 'What did you mean by what you just said?' she repeated.

'Oh, don't be silly, I was only teasing!' Bernice groaned, moving past the smaller woman to yank open the front door to the chauffeur. 'Why do you take everything so seriously?'

Even as she waved goodbye to her sister, Vivien was still finding it hard to get that uneasy snatch of dialogue out of her head. Possibly her sibling did know things about Lucca that his wife did not. Before bankruptcy had claimed her business, Bernice's boutique had been exceedingly fashionable and her rich clientele had often invited her to society parties. It was quite probable that when Lucca and Vivien had still been together Bernice would have heard rumours or tall stories about Lucca. However, Vivien, who had recently learned such a hard lesson in that particular field, had no intention of even allowing herself to consider the existence of any such allegations.

Within an hour of her arrival in London, she discovered that the label of furnished accommodation could hide a literal wealth of understatement, for her new home turned out to be a substantial dwelling in one of London's most exclusive suburbs. A beautiful flower arrangement greeted her in the hallway of the elegant detached house. Each room was so well set up for immediate occupation that at any moment she expected the real owners to arrive and ask her what she was doing there. But it was her own books that sat on the shelves in the study, her clothes that had been stowed in the handsome master bedroom and Marco's cot already awaited his arrival in the delightful nursery. Even the kitchen was well stocked with food. Having whined inconsolably for most of the journey, Jock scrambled out of the carrier box, his tail at a jaunty angle, and went trotting off to explore the secluded back garden.

The phone rang and, after a moment's hesitation, Vivien answered it.

'Give me a frank opinion,' Lucca invited smoothly.

His rich, dark drawl sent a little frisson of wicked awareness dancing down her sensitive spine and she clutched the phone as tight as a talisman. 'It's a wonderful house...but a lot bigger and fancier than I was expecting.'

'Staff have been organised to come in at discreet hours and take care of the necessities of life.'

'That would be ridiculously extravagant. I'll manage fine,' Vivien assured him earnestly.

At the other end of the line, Lucca almost winced. He was recalling the disastrous period after their honeymoon when Vivien had contrived to persuade him that she was personally capable of running the whole domestic show. His once comfortable existence had been replaced by the hair-raising thrills and spills and deprivation of Vivien's absent-minded brand of occasional housekeeping. The fire alarm had acted as an oven timer. The fridge had either been empty or filled with mummified food. The dry-cleaning had never been picked up. And sometimes, because she'd forgotten where she had left them, suits would vanish for all time. The most reliable way of acquiring a clean shirt had been the stack of new ones he kept at the office.

'I'm afraid there isn't a choice. The staff go with the house,' Lucca informed her. 'What time does Marco hit the bath?'

Vivien beamed. 'Seven…'

'I'll be there, *cara*.'

Lucca tossed the phone aside and lounged back against his desk with a feeling of intense satisfaction. Marco was in London…Vivien too. The one could not be got without the other, he reasoned lazily. A slow, wicked smile played over his hard, sensual mouth. Everything was going his way and why should it not? He had been born devious for good reason and smooth, perfect planning always paid off.

Vivien had intended to change into something a little fancier before Lucca arrived. Indeed for what remained of the afternoon, while cheerfully engaged in rearranging the nursery to her own satisfaction and playing with Marco, she strove to work out which outfits in her wardrobe most flattered her. From that dismally small selection she then endeavoured to decide which would strike that all-important note of careless indifference to male presence. The very last thing she wanted to risk was giving Lucca cause to suspect that she might have made a special effort to look good for his benefit.

As it happened, she didn't get the chance to change out of her casual low-slung black corduroy trousers and lilac tee shirt. An evening meal had been left prepared in the fridge for them but Marco disliked salads and he grizzled so much that Vivien ended up making him something else. Although the larder was well stocked, it did not carry any of Marco's favourite foods. By the time that Vivien managed to serve up toast and a boiled egg with the consistency of a bullet, her son was in a very cranky mood. Seated in his high chair, Marco refused to be hurried and kept on tossing down pieces of toast to an appreciative Jock.

'Don't do that,' Vivien urged for about the sixth time and struggled to be really firm. 'You're teaching Jock very bad manners,' she added, thinking that perhaps it would help if she explained why such behaviour was unacceptable. 'Marco, please hurry up and finish your egg...I want to get changed!'

Ignoring her, Marco waved his toast at Jock and the little dog danced round the high chair.

'Please don't do that...' Vivien urged plaintively, glancing at her watch with a groan of frustration because Lucca was due to arrive at any minute and he was never late.

Marco bumped his hand on the edge of the tray and accidentally let go of his toast. Jock snatched this unexpectedly generous offering from mid-air and raced off with his booty. Marco let out a roar of disbelief. 'Mine!' he yelled at the top of his voice.

At breathtaking speed that minor event built into a major incident. Marco was tired and cross and in a new house and, instead of instantly rushing to replace his toast, his mother lifted him out of his high chair and tried to fob him off with a piece of hastily buttered bread. He threw the bread on the floor. Jock took that too. It was the ultimate insult. In a tempestuous rage, Marco flung himself down on the tiles and screamed and kicked.

Vivien flipped herself upside down and walked on

her hands in a desperate attempt to distract her son. 'Look at Mummy, Marco!'

Letting himself into the house with his key, Lucca had a glossy perfect image in his mind of what life might have been like had Vivien not destroyed their marriage. His dream family composed of a smiling, elegant wife and a smiling son would have rushed to greet him whenever he came home. What greeted him instead and banished all fantasy was a wall of awful noise, composed of a wildly barking dog and a child screeching at the top of his voice.

Lucca was unprepared for the less-than-cosy domestic scene awaiting him in the kitchen. Marco was throwing himself about the floor in a passionate tantrum. But what took Lucca most aback was the sight of Vivien frantically walking round their son on her hands like an acrobat while simultaneously begging the enraged toddler to stop screaming.

'Marco…*stop it*!' Lucca ordered with icy authority.

For an instant a shattering silence fell. In the very act of opening his mouth wide on another ear-splitting howl, Marco turned his head in astonishment to focus big brown eyes on his father. Jock, having dropped the bread in his mouth, was striving to sneak up on Lucca from the side and was within an ace of sinking his teeth into a trouser leg.

'*No*, Jock!' Lucca rapped out, and he proffered the definitive insult to a watchdog who prided himself on his ferocity and took no account whatsoever of his own diminutive size: Lucca just stepped over the little animal to go to Vivien's aid. Shamed, Jock slunk beneath the kitchen table.

Vivien, the last to note Lucca's unannounced arrival, was so startled by the sound of his commanding

voice coming out of nowhere that she collided with a
kitchen stool and lost her balance. Lucca snaked out
a fast hand to prevent the stool from toppling on her
and then helped her back up onto her bare feet.

'Oh, my goodness, you're early!' Vivien accused
with a dismay she could not hide, both hands initially
engaged in smoothing down her rumpled fair hair but
swiftly faltering as the full effect of Lucca, sheathed
in a black pinstripe designer business suit, took her
self-possession by storm.

He was drop-dead gorgeous. It wasn't her fault that
she was staring, she told herself helplessly. Staring
was the norm in Lucca's vicinity. He never failed to
attract female attention. Pure energy buzzed in the air
around him. His height and sleek, powerful build were
combined with an extraordinarily sensual grace of
movement. His bronzed skin was moulded over fabulous cheekbones, a strong masculine nose and an aggressive jaw line. The dark gold allure of his deep-set
eyes set below level black brows made her heart
bounce inside her chest like a rubber ball. He lived
and breathed raw sexuality.

'It's after seven,' Lucca imparted. 'Was there a par-
ticular reason why you were walking on your hands?'
Her brows pleated in apparent surprise at the question.
'Didn't you realise why I was doing that?'

Lucca looked apologetic. 'I must be very slow on
the uptake.'

'It's simple and usually very effective,' Vivien assured him with enthusiasm. 'When Marco gets in a
temper, I try to avert trouble by providing him with a
distraction.'

'You have a wonderfully innovative approach to

discipline,' Lucca remarked, his slumberous gaze narrowing below lush black lashes as he studied her.

The self-conscious colour in her cheeks only enhanced the brightness of her sea-green eyes. Her soft full lips were a rosy, pouting invitation to a male who had always loved her mouth. Standing very straight, she was breathing rapidly from her recent acrobatic exertions, firm little breasts thrusting pointed nipples against a tee shirt worn thin from frequent washing. Instantaneous lust gripped Lucca. Suddenly he felt hot as hell. For a millisecond, he fought his own powerful response, for he had planned to play it cool for the first visit at least. But at shocking speed that recollection sank in favour of a keen desire to live for the moment and his lean hand rose almost of its own volition to curve to her waist, which lay bare below the hem of the shrunken tee shirt.

'I don't like to be confrontational with Marco…if that's what you mean.' The feverish tension weighting the atmosphere lent Vivien's voice a slightly nervous squeak but the immediacy with which he had reached out to pull her closer ran like a quicksilver burst of energy through her veins.

'You still talk at the worst possible moments,' Lucca growled in husky reproof.

'Whereas you don't talk at all,' she mumbled.

'Open your mouth for me, *gioia mia*.'

The long, sure fingers spreading across her sleek midriff felt like a possessive brand and she trembled when his other hand eased into the shallow indentation of her back to press her into electrifying contact with his lean well-built frame. A shiver of excitement coursed through her tummy and a kernel of heat ignited. She looked up at him, green eyes luminous. He brought his marauding mouth down on hers, his tongue slashing a carnal path of desire across the sensitive interior of her mouth. Her body flamed into almost painful life, a breathy little sound of fervent response wrenched from low in her throat. Her knees shook under her and when he crushed her slight length to him with hungry masculine force, she clung.

'Wow…triple wow,' she framed unsteadily with shining eyes, wildly conscious of the bold masculine proof of his arousal against her hip, her breath coming shallow and fast.

Shimmering golden eyes flamed over her in a provocative promise of more sensual delights to come. 'I aim to please and I always deliver…'

A small hand yanked at Lucca's trouser leg. He glanced down with a frown just as his son, whose presence he had entirely forgotten, hauled himself up into standing position and gave him a huge welcoming smile.

'A Saracino to the backbone…he can't stand to be ignored,' Lucca commented in a tone of rueful recognition as he backed off a step and scooped Marco up into his arms. 'But he's got a lousy sense of timing.'

Vivien felt shell-shocked by the separation imposed on them by her son's interruption. An instant later, she was hot-cheeked with shame at the abandoned way she had responded to Lucca. Writhing with embarrassment, she did her utmost to avoid Lucca's keen gaze. He had just kissed her and she had gone up in a shower of sparks like a firework. He had to think she was sex-starved. Or desperate. Or very keen. As she had been saying the love word just two short days ago, she reckoned that the only way to behave around

Lucca was to be ultra casual and friendly. For all he knew these days she went around telling every bloke she met that she loved him. Inwardly she cringed. How had she been so naïve? He had once told her that he was programmed to take advantage of naïve people and it *had* sounded like a warning.

'Bath time,' she announced breezily and marched out to the hall and up the stairs, leaving Lucca to follow.

He hovered like a third wheel while she ran the water and fetched pyjamas for Marco. 'Bathing a child is such an ordinary event,' he remarked. 'But I must confess that it feels strange to be here with you both.'

'Try doing it seven nights a week and I guarantee you'll get over the strangeness,' Vivien told him with a rueful laugh.

'How often can I expect to be made welcome in the space of a week?'

Smooth brow furrowing, Vivien glanced up and was hurt by the sardonic cast of his lean, darkly handsome features. 'Every night of the week if you like. I'm not going to keep you and Marco apart...I know you feel that you've missed a lot with him and I want to make up for that.'

'You're being very generous.' Lucca wondered if it was a clever ploy meant to persuade him to again consider reinstating their marriage.

'When I was awkward about arrangements before, it wasn't part of a deliberate policy. I swear it wasn't...I just found it very, very hard to let go of Marco even for a few hours,' Vivien confessed in a rush. 'But I didn't appreciate what I was doing to you or see how unfair I was being until you made me think about it this week.'

'What do I have to do or not do in return for this new way forward to continue?'

'Nothing…*nothing*!' she emphasised, hurt by the cynical look of suspicion in his steady scrutiny.

His wariness subsiding, Lucca dropped down into an athletic crouch to help her keep Marco still for long enough to undress his wriggling, restless little body. 'Let me take care of all this.'

Surprised that he wanted to get that involved, Vivien warned, 'He'll get you all wet…'

Lucca shed his jacket, loosened his silk tie and removed his gold cuff-links. 'No problem…'

Watching Lucca test the temperature of the water before lowering Marco with care and confidence into the bath, Vivien bit back the warning that Marco was as slippery as an eel. 'I can see you've done this at least once before.'

'*Sì*. With my cousin Paola's children…maybe a couple of times,' he admitted.

Vivien was really surprised. 'I never would've dreamt that you had that much interest in kids.'

'I didn't have until Marco was born.' He sent her a wry look from below his glorious ebony lashes and her heart rocked inside her. 'Sometimes when I couldn't see him, I went to see my cousin's family instead.'

Her throat thickened. It was the perfect moment for Marco to pounce with glee on his fleet of miniature plastic boats and fish and create a diversion.

'Do you want me to go?' Vivien prompted uncomfortably, thinking that her own presence was scarcely necessary and might even be a source of annoyance.

'*Perché*…what for?' Lucca countered levelly. 'Right now, Marco is happier being shared than fought

over. Let's not inflict too many changes on him at
once, *cara*.'

Unlike Vivien, Lucca understood how much fun it
was to have the fish noisily attack the boats by air and
by sea and watch the boats fill up and sink. Marco was
overjoyed by his father's infinitely more energetic approach to bath time. Vivien was helplessly fascinated
by what she was seeing: Lucca happily playing games
that would have not shamed a five-year-old and getting
splashed and soaked without complaint. The smiles
and the laughter that broke out with such frequency
only underlined the self-evident fact that Marco and
his father got on like a house on fire.

A raw smile of appreciation slashed Lucca's extravagantly handsome features as his son stretched up
trusting arms to be lifted out of the water. 'He's fantastic…'

The bold charisma of that smile and the warm, unashamed emotion in Lucca's stunning eyes made
Vivien's heart lurch. 'I think so too.'

Between them, Marco's wriggles were subdued for
long enough to get him wrapped into a fleecy towel.
Brilliant dark golden eyes assailed hers over the top
of the little boy's damp curly head. '*Dio mio*. You'd
have been pregnant at the altar if I'd known how much
I was likely to enjoy being a father!'

'Really?' She went pink. It crossed her mind that
had he made that leap in comprehension while she was
pregnant they might never have parted. But she didn't
say that because his unashamed love for Marco
touched her deep. She was seeing a gentler side to
Lucca's tough temperament than he had ever allowed
her, or, she imagined, most people, to see.

'You've done a fabulous job with him too,' Lucca breathed with blunt appreciation.

She was caught unprepared by that praise from a male to whom criticism came more readily, and Vivien's fair skin turned a deeper pink. Staring up at Lucca, she felt breathless and on a high and it was a second or two before she registered that that irritating repetitive noise in the background was actually the front doorbell ringing.

'Gosh, I'd better answer that...' With pronounced reluctance, she backed away and bumped her hip on the doorframe on her way out. 'I'll only be a minute.'

As she hurried down the stairs her thoughts were centred entirely on Lucca. Already his cool detachment and bitterness were taking a backseat. Didn't that prove that she had been right to agree the move to London? Her generosity was being rewarded. Lucca was smiling at her, complimenting her. They didn't have anything to fight about any more either! Wasn't that truly wonderful? A big sunny smile on her face, Vivien opened the front door.

Bewilderment held her still when Fabian Garsdale stepped into the porch. He was of medium height with distinguished wings of grey in his dark hair, and his neat metal-framed spectacles made him look very much like the academic he was.

'Fabian...my goodness, I wasn't expecting you.'

'The train fare cost me a small fortune.' His pale blue eyes were irritable. 'And I didn't get a seat.'

'Oh, dear, how very unfortunate,' Vivien soothed, struggling to silence Jock and prevent him from nipping playfully at Fabian's heels. Sadly, Fabian wasn't very doggy-orientated and Jock was forever teasing him. She shut the little animal into the kitchen and showed her visitor into the drawing room.

'Did you get my letter?' she asked.

Fabian had been away at a two-day conference in Hamburg. His absence had put her in a difficult position. She had not liked to break the news of her planned move in a phone call and he disliked email that was not work-related, so she had compromised by leaving a letter in his college pigeon-hole.

'How else would I have known where you were? I set off as soon as I read it. I think that you've been very rash,' he informed her with a reproving shake of his head.

Vivien never liked it when Fabian spoke to her as though she were a not-very-bright four-year-old but he spoke to virtually everybody that way. 'In the circumstances, I didn't feel I had much choice.'

'I wish that you had phoned me to discuss this course of action before you agreed to it,' Fabian complained rather shortly. 'It's admirable that you should want to achieve a more civilised relationship with Marco's father and enable him to take greater responsibility for his son. But you must be sensible and consider your own future as well.'

'It wasn't possible to do both…or, at least, where Lucca and Marco are concerned, things are rather more complex than that,' she extended awkwardly, for, while her letter to Fabian had been as frank as their friendship deserved, she had not revealed anything very personal about the current state of her relationship with Lucca.

'Of course they are. Naturally that silly woman's newspaper confession opened old wounds but you

mustn't forget that you are practically divorced,'
Fabian pointed out testily.

Vivien lost colour at that reminder. 'I'll be divorced
when it's final.'

'I can see that you still need to get Lucca Saracino
out of your system.' Fabian compressed his thin lips
and raised a brow at the surprise blossoming in her
expressive face. 'I'm not a fool, Vivien. I don't suffer
from jealousy either. I'm a very pragmatic man.
Before this happened, our friendship was moving onto
a new stage. I was planning to ask you to marry me
once you were free. However, recent events have su-
perseded that time frame.'

Vivien was startled by that calm announcement of
intent, for she had been quite unaware that the older
man had begun thinking of her as a potential wife.
'Fabian…I don't know what to say. I had no—'

'No, this is not the time to give me an answer,'
Fabian decreed with slight impatience. 'It's merely important that you should know that that option is there
for the future. I have great respect and affection for
you and we work very well together. I don't know
much about children but I would do my best to be a
good stepfather to your son.'

A lump formed in her throat. She was touched and
felt that she must have been shockingly blind not to
notice the extent of his attachment to her. 'How long
have you been in love with me?' she asked in an apologetic whisper.

'Good heavens, no! I haven't got quite that carried
away.' Fabian laughed out loud at that idea. 'I hope I
have more sense!'

Vivien froze. 'Oh…then why were you thinking of
marrying me?'

'I find your company pleasant. You're not a demanding woman. You have a remarkable brain,' he acknowledged with his first hint of enthusiasm. 'Mother likes you too. Her disliking you would not have prevented me from proposing but it would have made life difficult.'

The emotive lump in Vivien's throat had wholly dissolved. It seemed that even her brain had more pulling power than the rest of her. Of course he didn't love her. Nobody had ever really loved her but Marco. And she should have known better than to ask such a stupid question. Fabian was more into research than passion. In truth, he was not much given to emotion and his sense of humour was slight, but he was sincere. It was perfectly possible that he felt more for her in his dry, prosaic way than Lucca had ever felt for her, she thought wretchedly.

'I'm pleased that your mother liked me,' Vivien muttered tightly.

'She has excellent taste.' Fabian checked his watch. 'I'm afraid I can't stay any longer. I did promise to call in with a friend while I was in town. I'll keep in touch. In due course, I expect you'll be in a better position to give me a considered response to my proposal.'

As Fabian held open the door into the hall for her Vivien wondered if she ought to be thanking him for proposing, because it seemed awful to say nothing at all, and then she heard herself saying instead, 'You know…Lucca's here right now. He's upstairs with Marco.'

'I think not…' Fabian said drily, drawing her attention belatedly to the tall dark male striding down the stairs.

'Where's Marco?' Vivien asked Lucca anxiously, noting that he had replaced his tie and jacket. Apart from the fact that his luxuriant black hair was sexily tousled, he looked as sophisticated and bone-deep cool as always.

'Fast asleep in his cot.' Lucca surveyed Fabian with brooding intensity. He wasn't that bad-looking for a short, skinny guy of advanced years. 'You must be Fabian…'

'Garsdale…Professor.' Fabian extended a polite hand.

'Must you leave so soon?' Lucca purred and the silence was like a whirlpool gathering speed and destructive force.

Fabian stepped out rather hurriedly onto the doorstep. 'Unfortunately, I must. I'm afraid I have another appointment and I'm running rather late as it is.'

'What was he doing here?' Lucca demanded harshly the instant the door closed on Fabian's exit.

Vivien fell still, a dangerous light brightening the sadness in her eyes. 'Fabian came here to tell me that he wanted to marry me,' she admitted quietly.

'Ha…bloody…ha,' Lucca pronounced, unimpressed.

Anger came out of nowhere and roared through Vivien like an energising tidal wave. 'Do you have a problem believing that another man might value me enough to ask me to be his wife?'

CHAPTER SEVEN

'No, I don't have a problem crediting that someone else might propose to you,' Lucca drawled, smooth as glass. 'I did it myself once.'

Vivien flinched. It was an injudicious reminder that summoned up memories of one of the most wonderful days of her life and made her all too miserably aware of how far they had travelled from that point. Three years had passed since Lucca had flown her to France to watch one of his racehorses win at Longchamp. Afterwards, he had proposed over champagne and strawberries and an exquisite diamond ring had been slid onto her finger. She had been so happy she'd cried.

'I bet you wish you hadn't,' Vivien said facetiously.

'I could never *un*wish Marco—'

'But when I was carrying him, you would've done like a shot!'

'I refuse to rise to that bait. We both made wrong assumptions on that score—'

'You just can't admit even now that you might have been in the wrong,' Vivien condemned britily.

His wide, sensual mouth compressed. 'Let's concentrate on Professor Garsdale. Did he *really* ask you to marry him?' Lucca enquired, as though that were quite the weirdest and very possibly the most comic thing he had heard since time began.

Vivien jerked her chin in stiff acknowledgement. 'I fail to see why that should amuse you.'

'Do I seem amused?' The glitter of gold in Lucca's stunning gaze was bright as the heart of a fire. 'You have got me wrong. I'm astonished by Garsdale's nerve and surprised you didn't throw him out of the house. Or was his short stay the result of your request that he leave?'

Her teeth gritted together. 'Most women would regard a marriage proposal as a compliment. I can't see why you would think I'd be tempted to show Fabian the door over the head of it!'

'You must be very obtuse.'

'I don't think so. You're being incredibly rude.' Vivien could hear her own voice rising in spite of her desire to remain cool in the face of all provocation. 'Fabian is very respected in academic circles and he has been a very good friend to me.'

'He also happens to be easily old enough to be your father. Possibly you have reached the conclusion that I was a little *too* exciting for you,' Lucca murmured, offering that tantalising opinion in a drawl as soft as silk. 'But opting for the equivalent of a quiet space in a twin coffin seems rather premature for a woman who is only twenty-seven years old.'

The burn effect of his whiplash tongue sent a painful flush climbing up Vivien's slender throat. 'I suppose you think it's clever to be smart at Fabian's expense.'

'Don't you find it strange that the professor left you here alone with me without a murmur?'

'Fabian is too mature and too dignified to stoop to any other kind of behaviour!'

Lucca vented a not very pleasant laugh. 'Is that what you call it? I would have said his hasty departure had much more to do with self-preservation. He didn't want to risk a scene and he didn't want to rile me either.'

Vivien thrust up her chin, her anger steadily mounting. 'You've got no right to imply that Fabian might be a coward.'

His brilliant golden gaze was heavily sardonic. 'Stop trying to send me up, Vivi. You wouldn't even consider marrying a guy like that after me!'

'Oh, wouldn't I?' The sound of that pet name was like salt rubbed in an open wound. Once that name had been a term of affection and intimacy. Now it was only a cruel *aide-mémoire* to all she had lost. She honestly did not know how she had been tempted into the indiscretion of telling Lucca that Fabian had asked her to marry him. But having done it, she would have loyally defended Fabian to the death. Lucca's derisive remarks only added a more bitter edge to emotions that were already threatening to get out of her control.

His lean, strikingly handsome face clenched hard. 'No, you wouldn't marry him,' he breathed almost harshly, answering his own arrogant question. 'You deserve better than a guy I can laugh at.'

'Sticks and stones. You're so wrong about Fabian!' Vivien slung him a tempestuous look of condemnation, dimly wondering why she was so angry with him. 'I don't think he would ever make me as unhappy as you did—'

An ebony brow elevated, questioning that statement. 'I doubt that very much. You're full of passion and he acts like a very cold fish.'

'When I was no longer flavour of the month, there was nobody colder than you. Fabian isn't volatile and it's highly unlikely that anyone will *ever* refer to him as a womaniser!'

'*Inferno!* I am not and I have never been a womaniser.' Lucca swore, slashing a lean brown hand through the air in fierce emphasis. 'I resent the label. I have a high public profile. If I'm even seen talking to a woman, the rumour that I've bedded her hits the gossip columns. When we got married, I became even more of a target.'

Vivien flung her head back, rumpled golden hair tumbling round her flushed cheekbones. 'Is Bliss Masterson just a rumour?' she flung at him, knowing even as she spoke that she should not say it but still saying it regardless.

'I do not owe you an explanation for anything I've done since *you* walked out on our marriage!' Lucca raked back at her, enraged at the rank injustice of that gibe.

Vivien folded her arms in a defensive movement, upped her chin another aggressive notch and scanned him with furious green eyes that concealed her hurt. 'Well, actually, I think you do because, like it or not, you've still been married to me for the past two years!'

'*Sì...*' Lucca sent her a slashing look of angry derision. 'One of the greatest ironies is that you ended our marriage over an act of infidelity that never happened and in that clever way ensured that I've been unfaithful ever since!'

Vivien unfroze from the energising rage that had momentarily blocked out all but the disturbing highly charged surge of her own confused emotions. She went from rage to pain in the blink of an eyelid. She felt like someone snatched from a sauna and plunged into icy snow. Shockwaves coursed through her because she was finally being forced to face a reality she had consistently refused to acknowledge: Lucca's ongoing sexual infidelity and the other women in his life. For the two years of their separation, she had been careful never to open a newspaper that might carry stories about her estranged husband's social life. After all, why should she have tormented herself with information that could only upset her? Living with the wounding conviction that Lucca had made love to the voluptuous Jasmine Bailey had surely been punishment enough.

His lean, strong face was clenched hard. 'I'm sorry…that crack was out of order and unproductive.'

But it was too late. The comforting cocoon of ignorance that Vivien had inhabited for two years had been blown wide open to the unkind elements. Now the howling wind and the battering rain were ripping a giant hole in her self-possession. How could she have been so blind that she refused to face how much had changed between them? Yet on the day that Jasmine Bailey's revelations had been published, she had rushed to London in an effort to save their marriage. She had behaved as if the intervening two years had not happened. Two years during which Lucca, shorn of the inhibiting factor of a loyal and loving wife, had contrived to be as unfaithful with other women as he had *not* been with Jasmine Bailey. He was quite correct, she reflected heavily: there was an excruciating irony to that horrible truth.

'Vivi…?' Lucca breathed in a driven undertone, for she was as pale and distant from him as a victim of shock.

No wonder he had told her that day at his office to stop behaving like the Sleeping Beauty who had been stood up by her Prince. He had moved on from their broken marriage and returned to the life of a single male. He had enjoyed other relationships, slept with other women. But she had not had a single relationship since she had left Lucca. Her platonic friendship with Fabian looked quite pitiful when set next to Lucca's likely track record.

'I've never slept with anyone but you,' Vivien muttered with a dulled laugh empty of amusement. 'My goodness, what a boring person I must be!'

'I don't think that's boring…I think that kind of moral restraint is praiseworthy, *cara*,' Lucca hastened to assert, shifting instantly closer to reach for her clenched fingers.

'Even if you don't embrace it yourself?' Vivien prompted in a thin, tight tone, snatching her hand out of reach before he could touch it and widening the distance between them.

Lucca sidestepped that awkward question. 'I think you should be proud of your values. I am…very much.'

'I expect it's suited you. An estranged wife running round having affairs with all and sundry might have been rather embarrassing for a guy like you. Those values of mine have worked against my own interests most, haven't they?' At the back of her mind Vivien knew she was still avoiding the real issue of his infidelity because she did not want him to see her pain. Or even worse, tell her one more time that what he did with other women was none of her affair, for what could more clearly demonstrate that their marriage was as dead as he had said it was?

His level dark brows pleated. 'I don't see how.'

'I'd have got over you a lot quicker if I'd got involved with someone else. Obviously the fact that I *didn't* find someone else—'

'What about Fabian?' Lucca slotted in, getting

tenser by the second as the atmosphere escalated in response to the powerful emotional vibrations she was emanating.

'I haven't slept with him...yet,' she adjusted, wondering if she even wanted to share a bed with Fabian. She registered with a sinking heart that she did not have the slightest desire to sleep with Fabian and that therefore she could probably look forward to at least another sixty years of being alone. Bitterness assailing her at the longevity of her emotional attachment to Lucca, she finally attacked the subject she had been evading and she did so head-on and right in at the deep end. 'So, tell me...how many women have you slept with since we broke up?'

Something perilously akin to panic flashed through Lucca. It took a split second for him to appreciate what the sensation was because that dark sense of dread laced with fear was entirely new to his experience. Her conversational tone made the question hit all the harder. He knew he didn't want to answer the question. He knew that even one woman had been too many. He snatched in a slow, deep breath like a guy battening down the hatches in a storm and expecting the very worst nature could throw at him.

Vivien watched his gorgeous dark golden eyes veiling as if the shutters were being slammed. Colour accentuated his spectacular cheekbones. In a twisted way she rejoiced in his discomfiture. It went a very little way towards compensating for the agonising jealousy and despair that she was struggling to conceal from him. 'Aren't you going to answer me, Lucca?'

'No,' Lucca breathed tautly. 'I don't want you to get upset about this.'

Vivien stretched to her full, not very impressive

height much as if a poker had been welded to her backbone. Her green eyes took on a glassy brightness. 'My goodness, do I look upset?' she asked, a tad shrilly. 'I'm not that sensitive. You said you'd moved on and I'm just trying to move on too—'

'Too fast. Speed junkies crash.'

'Trying to frighten me off the subject? Do you think I *care* how many women you've slept with?' Vivien launched at him, a whole octave higher.

A thunderous silence spread. Lucca was very still and studiously quiet. Torture would not have dredged a look or a sound from him at that instant.

'I'm understanding a whole lot more about myself all of a sudden,' Vivien asserted, her hands coiling into tight fists by her sides. 'The biggest mistake I made was to go on thinking of myself as married when we were no longer living together. That's probably why I ended up in bed with you again as well.'

His strong jaw line squared. 'I don't think so, *gioia mia*. I think that resulted from something more than habit—'

'Well, I blasted well don't and it's a habit I'm going to outgrow faster than the speed of light!' Vivien swore vehemently. 'So, it would be of great assistance to me if you were to be honest now about how many women you have had in your life since I left you. It's called aversion therapy.'

'Santo Cielo!' Lean, extravagantly handsome features taut with disquiet, Lucca strode forward and reached for both her hands. 'Let's stop this in its tracks. It's pointless and destructive…you're tearing yourself apart—'

'I'm not half so sensitive as you seem to think!' Vivien dragged her fingers free in a fierce physical repudiation of his offer of support, for his approach had wounded her pride even more.

'OK…you're tearing *me* apart,' Lucca conceded in a raw undertone. 'Nothing I have done is worthy of one moment of your distress—'

'My life has overflowed with distress since I met you,' Vivien told him with a venom created by the awful hollow opening up inside her like a chasm. 'I've spent two years with my head buried in the sand. I wouldn't let myself think about what you were getting up to. Tell me…how long did you wait before you found someone else to fill that vacant space in our bed?'

'Vivi…*please*!' Lucca spread his arms wide in a gesture of violent frustration and strode over to the window, savage tension etched in every angular line of his big, powerful frame.

'No, I'm entitled to ask. I've decided that I'm not going to deal with feelings any more, but with cold, hard facts,' she declared wildly.

'But you're not a cold, hard person and I don't want you to be hurting.'

Her pointed face froze, her pallor pronounced. 'I'm not hurting…where did you get the idea that you still had the power to hurt me? You're everything I loathe in a man. I'll bet you've had a string of women and affairs but you still have the nerve to tell me that my old-fashioned values are praiseworthy!'

Lucca was unusually pale beneath his bronzed skin. 'Vivien—'

'I want you out of here right now!' Vivien gasped, because her throat was raw with tears and she was terrified of breaking down in front of him. 'You're welcome any time you choose to see Marco but I want you to give me that key you used to let yourself in tonight. When I start entertaining my male friends to cosy nights in, I won't want you walking in and embarrassing me!'

'What male friends…cosy nights in?' Lucca growled in a wrathful drawl utterly shorn of cool sophistication. 'Have you gone out of your mind?'

'No, I've finally come to my senses. Instead of looking back to our marriage like you are the only man in the world, I'm about to start living again!'

'You have this idea that I've been sleeping around—'

Vivien surged past him with prickling eyes and hauled open the front door in invitation. 'As far as I'm concerned, the day you climbed into a bed that did not contain me you died as a husband.' She stuck out a small hand. 'Key, please.'

Incensed and incredulous golden eyes locked into hers. 'Where's the woman who said she wanted me back at any cost?'

'How dare you throw that in my face?' Vivien practically sobbed at him, so desperate was she to get him to leave before she lost what little control remained to her.

'OK?' Lucca set the key down with measured precision on the window sill of the porch. 'Will you please calm down?'

'I don't need to calm down—'

'I don't want to leave when you're feeling like this—'

'What's wrong with the way I'm feeling?' Vivien demanded, with a choky indistinctness to her usually quiet voice. 'I'm feeling fabulous…free and ready to

grab my new life as a divorced woman the first chance
I get!'

'Will you phone me later?' Lucca pressed tautly.

'I'll be far too busy, and how would I call you anyway? Only your lovers have your mobile phone number!' Vivien gibed in a fevered burst of bitterness.

Lucca printed the number on the pad by the hall
phone.

'Please get out,' she urged between clenched teeth.

The door flipped shut on his departure, sealing her
into the silent house. She let Jock out of the kitchen
and clutched him so tight he yelped in complaint.
Apologising, she set him down again. In shock at the
force of her own emotions, she finally crept back upstairs and looked in on the nursery. Marco was asleep,
the twin ebony crescents of his lashes smooth on his
olive cheeks, one arm flung out with his little hand
open in complete relaxation. A great sob started building up inside her and she hurtled into the bathroom
where a trio of discarded nappies let her know how
much trouble Lucca had had dealing with that necessity. Choking back sobs, she told herself that she
should have guessed that Lucca's much-vaunted fond-
ness for the company of young children would have
entailed little experience at the sharper end of child-
care.

She stared into space. Tears were running down her
face in rivulets. She sniffed and gulped. Funny how
she had not been able to wait to get him out of the
house but the instant he had gone she was tormented
by her aloneness. Yet she had Marco and she reminded
herself that many people had a lot less. Yes, she had
Marco to love. Don't think about Lucca and beds and
fantastically beautiful women like Bliss Masterson...

All the feelings that she had been too craven to deal with were crowding in on her now. When she fondly imagined that she could put their marriage back together, she had been living her own little fairy tale and fighting to have a happy ending. Lucca had made love to her again and she had reasoned that that had to mean something. But hadn't she once read somewhere that couples on the brink of divorce often did end up back in bed together at least once? It hadn't meant anything to Lucca: he had even said so. Just sex. Just a meaningless, mindless thing...

The phone was ringing. She stumbled into the bedroom to answer it.

'May I come back in?' Lucca enquired flatly.

She squeezed her sore eyes tight shut. 'No...'

'I feel like hell...you're upset. I should be with you.'

'No...no, you shouldn't be,' Vivien framed jaggedly and she put the phone down again.

The walls of the room felt as if they were closing in on her. She opened the door out onto the small balcony that overlooked the back garden and dragged in a great gulp of the cool evening air. When the phone began ringing again, she walked out of the bedroom and closed the door on it. But phones were ringing downstairs as well. She sank down on a step halfway down the handsome staircase. What foolish threats she had flung at Lucca! He wasn't in love with her. How would it upset him if she slept with other men?

A tempest of emotion was storming her. He was the guy she loved but she couldn't have him. She didn't want to see him, knew she shouldn't let herself see him. How was she supposed to get over him when he wouldn't leave her alone to grieve? She had to be braver, stronger. Surrendering to a spiteful desire to make him feel bad would do her no good at all.

The bell on the front door shrilled an unmistakable call and when she ignored it, the knocker went instead. Irritated beyond bearing, she leapt up, raced down the stairs and shouted through the door, 'I hate you!'

Her voice snapped in the middle like a bendy twig and she wondered if he too had heard that all too audible sound of weakness through the thickness of the wood door separating them. Biting back another tempestuous sob, she retreated hurriedly into the hall again. She did not want him to realise that she was crying.

On the other side of the solid door, Lucca swore long and low and fiercely. He should never have given that key back! Somehow he had to get back into the house even if it meant breaking in. Light was pouring down from the balcony at the side of the house. Lucca groaned when he saw the door left open up there like a mocking invitation. All his life he had fought his fear of heights. It was his biggest, darkest secret.

He got into his McLaren F1 and reversed it to below the balcony. He got up on the roof of the car. It was an old house with high ceilings and he still had a good way to climb. Edging across the slippery car roof, he grasped a hold of the sturdy ivy trunk growing up the wall. He snatched in a shuddering breath. He knew his fear was irrational. He was barely six feet off the ground but it felt like twenty. In a cold sweat, he hauled himself up. Jock hurtled out of the house, literally bouncing on his three legs with every frantic, explosive bark.

'Shut it!' Lucca warned him.

Jock growled, a long, deep, threatening growl that would not have shamed a Rottweiler about to attack.

Lucca reached for the stone parapet and dragged himself over it. Clumsy with eagerness, he misjudged his step and landed hard enough on the tiled floor to jar every bone in his powerful body. Jock jumped on top of him like a Victorian big-game hunter posing for a triumphant photograph.

Vivien was curled up in a ball on the bottom step of the stairs, still and silent and small. 'Vivi...' he breathed tautly to lessen the shock of his appearance.

In disbelief, she twisted round and vaulted upright. 'Lucca...?'

'I was worried about you. I came in by the balcony. 'Lucca strode down the stairs, intense golden eyes locking to her pale tear-streaked face and lingering.

She could think of nothing to say. She trembled, tried to shrug and, without any warning whatsoever, he just hauled her into his arms and brought his mouth crashing down on her full, soft lips, demanding and receiving a response that was equally fierce.

He crushed her to him, spread long fingers either side of her face and let his sensual mouth rove from her unmarked brow to her delicate eyelids and the petal softness of her cheeks before closing with hungry, passionate fervour to her parted lips again.

'We mustn't...' she mumbled in a daze.

Shimmering dark golden eyes ensnared hers with unashamed purpose. 'We *must*...'

CHAPTER EIGHT

'BLISS…?' Vivien whispered uncertainly, anxious green eyes pinned to Lucca's lean, strong face.

Lucca vented a harsh laugh. 'It was over with her the first time I held you in my arms again. I had a fever only you could quench, *gioia mia*.'

Vivien breathed again. 'I'm glad…' How glad, she was too choked up to tell him. It was an effort to think when she simply wanted to glory in him. He was holding her so tightly that she could barely feed air into her lungs. Even though he was crushing her, she made no complaint, for she craved that intensity with every fibre of her being.

With a husky sound of all-male satisfaction, Lucca bent down and swept her slight body up into his powerful arms. 'While I'm with you, there will be nobody else·in my life,' he delivered with hard clarity. 'That is how it always was and I don't change.'

There was an unspoken rebuke in that declaration. That was the moment that she knew she had to say goodbye to the past if it was not to destroy the present. He was an all-or-nothing guy and, two years ago, she had let him down. She had walked out on their marriage instead of staying to fight for it and the truth. She had to accept that in leaving she had given Lucca his freedom back. He had not put his life on ice, he had gone on living, and what right did she have to complain about that? She had judged him unfairly, denied him any right of appeal and her lack of trust had outraged his sense of justice. Her thoughtless limitations on the time he got to spend with Marco had only increased his bitterness, adding to the barriers he had put up against her. But one by one those barriers were falling and that was all, absolutely all that really mattered, she told herself feverishly. The second chance she had prayed for had been granted and she was not going to be ungrateful for it.

Halfway up the stairs, Lucca paused to plunder the swollen pink welcome of her ripe mouth. He had never felt a hunger so intense. He needed to be with her. He was with her. He refused to think beyond that as he laid her down on the bed. 'Vivi…' he breathed in a throaty tone that made her ache.

'I'm glad you wouldn't take no for an answer,' she whispered, her voice gruff from the amount of crying she had done.

His gorgeous eyes were darker than the sky on a stormy night. He lifted a not-quite-steady lean brown hand and let long, lean fingers score very lightly down one soft cheek. 'When I want something, I go for it, *cara mia.*'

'Don't stop wanting me,' she muttered, taut as a bowstring.

'You'd have to tell me *how*…' Lucca confided in a roughened drawl.

'I will hardly do that.' Energised by that admission of his, she sat up and began, with all the awkwardness of someone who had never taken on such a role before, to slide his jacket off his wide shoulders.

His bold gaze locked to hers, he shrugged out of the jacket in a fluid, sexy movement. Breathing in deep, emboldened by partial success, she embarked on his tie with hands that felt infuriatingly clumsy. 'I'm not very good at this,' she warned him.

'You can practise on me as often as you like, but tonight such refinements would be wasted on me,' Lucca asserted huskily, discarding his tie and ripping at his shirt with unashamed impatience. With it hanging loose to reveal a muscular bronzed slice of hair-roughened chest, he scooped her off the mattress to stand her up between his spread thighs.

His expert mouth claiming hers in a series of tantalising rough and then soft kisses stole her concentration. The faint drag of his teeth on her soft, full lower lip and the thrust of his tongue made her shiver in sensual shock and gasp. Meanwhile, almost without her knowledge and certainly without her input, she was being undressed. Her corduroy jeans were shimmied down over her slender hips, but she had no idea where they went after that because what Lucca was doing to her mouth was a wicked enticement of her every sense.

'I love your mouth,' he groaned, soft as silk, his breath fanning the smooth skin of her midriff as he bent his dark head to trail a soothing kiss there before he eased up the tee shirt over her narrow ribcage. 'I love your skin…but most of all I love to look at you, *bella mia*.'

'I don't know why…' she said shyly as he drew her down to him.

His dark golden eyes arrowed with lingering masculine appreciation over the pale pouting thrust of her small rose-tipped breasts. 'For me…you are perfection,' he breathed thickly. 'Chemistry like this doesn't die just because you want it to.'

'Did you want it to?' Vivien whispered, hurt by that concept.

Lucca gave her a stunned look of incomprehension. *'Che altro*...what else? When you left me, of course I wanted my hunger for you to die. It was like you had taken half of me away as well,' he countered in a roughened undertone. 'How was I to live like that?'

Her heart twisted inside her. Moisture prickled the back of her eyes and her throat hurt. But before she could think about what she'd just learned when she'd least expected to, Lucca tangled one hand into the fall of her pale golden hair and ravished her mouth with a raw, explosive passion that left her dizzy.

He smoothed possessive hands over her sensitive breasts and she shivered. He let his thumbs play in gentle, teasing circles over the tender buds eager for his attention. Heat lay coiled like a river of fire at the core of her. Her hips shifted up in a tiny rising motion. The ache of want began then, at first lending a delicious, bittersweet edge to response but minute by minute he pushed back the boundaries until the extent of her own anticipation made patience impossible.

The skim of his tongue over her delicate skin made her twist and whimper. He scored a light, knowing fingertip over the taut, damp triangle of fabric stretched tight between her thighs. Suddenly she was hotter than she could bear and pushing up against him with eagerness and a longing beyond anything she had ever felt in her life before.

'Lucca...' Stretching up, she found his handsome mouth again all on her own and tasted him. A pulse beat of restive desire was taking her by storm.

With an earthy sound low in his throat, he drew up her legs and peeled off her panties. He stroked the wet silk heart of her, established his welcome and she moaned out loud, unable to stay still. Again she reached up to let the pink tip of her tongue flicker across the outline of his wide, sensual lips and then dip between, driven by the shameless craving to urge him on.

'I surrender, *bella mia*,' Lucca growled, pressing her slim shoulders flat to the pillows, lean, strong face stamped with raw, male hunger.

'Don't make me wait,' she whispered, taken aback by her own daring, but controlled by a need that was too tormenting for her to fight.

'I couldn't...' A stormy flash of fierce elemental gold flared in his arresting gaze. Lifting himself back from her, he unzipped his well-cut trousers. His rampant arousal was clearly delineated by the fine expensive fabric. Her face was hot as he came back to her. All male and licensed to be impatient, he parted her thighs and found his place with a ground-out sigh of satisfaction. 'Night after night, you've haunted my dreams, and now I'm living my wildest fantasy, *gioia mia*.'

He shifted with pure masculine provocation to acquaint her with his raw male power. In a bold movement, wholly attuned to the dominance that she yearned for in that instant, he plunged hard into the slick, tight depths of her. The pleasure was immediate, overwhelming. She jerked, her spine arching as she loosed a low, keening cry.

'Is it good?' Lucca stared down at her with a blaze of primitive satisfaction in his assessing scrutiny of her delicate pointed face. 'I want it to be so good you can't stay away from me.'

'Lock me up…throw away the key!' she gasped wildly.

'No, *bella mia*,' He shifted his lean hips in a smooth circling motion, teasing her with his strength and control. 'You know the rules. You must choose of your own free will to be with me.'

'I choose…oh, I *choose* to be with you,' she framed, shakily but fiercely.

Shoulder muscles bulging, he swooped down to claim a devouring kiss that sent the blood racing at breakneck speed through her veins. She felt possessed on every level and it was the most electrifying sensation that she had ever known. Then he lifted his arrogant dark head again. His exotic dark golden eyes raked over her with savage approval.

He sank into her deeper and faster. She arched up to him in surrender and welcome. In a breathless urgent gasp, she cried his name. The roller coaster of breakneck excitement was racing through her again. The ache of tormented hunger swelled, driving her on out of control to a shattering peak she had never touched before. The equivalent of a rocket display took off inside her. She hit the heights of ecstasy and then swan-dived down and down and down onto the mental equivalent of a fluffy feather bed. She felt as if she could fly, but the reassuring weight of Lucca's big, powerful body held her entrapped.

Being trapped had never felt so good. He hugged her close with the easy affection that had once been so natural between them. Happiness engulfed her and she strung an exuberant line of kisses along one wide bronzed shoulder before carefully following suit along the other. Lucca smiled into the tumbled silk of her hair, breathing in the fresh, clean, camomile scent of it. He found her hands and held them both tight and then lifted one lazily to his indolent mouth and pressed a single gentle kiss to her palm.

'Vivi…' he murmured softly.

'I want you to know that I chose you a long time ago,' Vivien murmured eagerly.

His lean, powerful length tensed almost imperceptibly. His tousled dark head came up, the brilliance of his gaze enhanced by the density of his inky lashes. 'Try not to forget that you also chose to ditch me when the going got tough.'

Vivien lost colour. 'I didn't…it wasn't like that!'

'So watch out, *bella mia*,' Lucca breathed, smoother than silk sliding on silk. 'Next time, I'll do the ditching.'

Her glowing happiness died as if someone had switched off an interior light. She turned her head away.

Lucca studied her forlorn aspect with the intensity of a highly suspicious male. She looked so quiet and acted so shy and undemanding. He would have been prepared to swear that she had not a devious bone in her tiny body. But somehow, when it came to getting her own way, she was the equivalent of an armoured battering ram. She could be terrifyingly effective and he had never yet worked out how she achieved her results.

Her unsung triumphs were many more than she would ever guess. When he had first asked her out, he had only wanted an affair, but he had been hooked into an exclusive arrangement straight off and choosing a diamond ring by the next full moon. Shattered by the speed of his own capitulation, he had planned to stay engaged for years and years. However, her refusal to move in with him had sent wedding bells flying to the top of his agenda. When he'd said he was too busy to take a honeymoon, she'd said that if he was returning to work immediately, so must she and, oh, yes, by the way…she would have to do a two-week-long stint with students at some remote cottage in the chilly Scottish Highlands. He had arranged the honeymoon the same day. All those subtle feminine victories in mind, Lucca levered himself back from her, sprang off the bed and strode into the bathroom.

He was about to get in the shower when Vivien entered the bathroom.

'So do it now,' she told him curtly.

Lucca frowned in sincere incomprehension. 'Do… *what*?'

'Ditch me.' Sea-green eyes challenged him. 'Go ahead…I'm waiting.'

'But I don't want to ditch you!' Lucca spelt out, sardonic as he could be.

'Then, Lucca…I'll do it for you,' Vivien countered, sweeter than saccharine in tone. 'You're ditched.'

'*Dannazione!* What are you playing at?' Lucca raked at her with wrathful incredulity.

'I don't like threats. Don't you dare talk about ditching me just because I made the mistake of letting you into my bed again!' Vivien warned him hotly.

With another bitten-back swear word, Lucca yanked a towel from the rail and knotted it round his lean hips. He thrust spread fingers through his cropped black hair, which would have been as luxuriantly curly as his son's had he not kept it short. 'I was teasing you…'

Fingernails biting painful crescents into her palm, Vivien stood her ground. 'If I drove you to the edge of a cliff and abandoned you above a thousand-foot drop, would you consider that "teasing"?'

Dark blood flared over his fabulous cheekbones. 'Who told you I didn't like heights?'

'Your sister.' Vivien winced, her lovely face taking on a guilty cast. 'I'd never have let you know I knew if you hadn't said what you did. Especially not after you were so incredibly brave climbing up onto the balcony.'

Lucca endeavoured to hang onto his grim expression and failed. She had hit back at him and now she was beating herself up for it. A wicked grin chased the bleak aspect and tugged at the corners of his beautiful mouth. 'Are you going to tell people? Hold it over me every time I annoy you?'

Vivien slowly shook her fair head. 'I wouldn't do that to you.'

Lucca closed his hands over hers and tugged her close. 'For just a minute or two, being with you again spooked me, *bella mia*.'

As in once burned, twice shy? As in, I can't stick this woman? As in, What on earth am I doing with her again? A frantic need to know exactly what he had meant by that word 'spooked' gripped Vivien. But it was not the time to subject him to an interrogation.

'It's been a very emotional evening,' she conceded.

Slumberous heat flamed in his golden appraisal. 'We need to relax,' he told her, untying the wrap she had put on and trailing it off.

'Lucca!' she gasped.

'If you think that is shocking...' gorgeous eyes glinting, he dropped his towel '...wait until you see what I can get up to in the shower.'

Around dawn he eased out of bed without waking

her and pulled on his clothes. Hooking his jacket over
his finger, he surveyed her peaceful profile. Fabian
Garsdale was surely out of the picture now. He strolled
across the landing, surveyed his sleeping son with immense pride and went downstairs. Jock whined from
behind the kitchen door. Lucca hesitated and then suppressed a groan.

Jock was just waiting to pounce. It took some pretty
nifty footwork to prevent the little terrier getting in a
nip and, frustrated by his lack of success, Jock pulled
his falling-over stunt. Lucca located the biscuit tin and
extracted a chocolate biscuit, which he wafted above
the still animal. Scrambling up, Jock displayed amazing powers of recovery and snatched at the biscuit.
When the biscuit remained out of reach, he uttered a
bark of furious protest.

'We have to come to a deal,' Lucca told his tor-
mentor, squatting down to meet defiant black eyes set
in a shock of long, dusty dark hair. Lucca was reminded of an aggressive floor mop. 'A deal that in-
volves bribery and corruption in return for my safe
passage. Here…'

Bristling with distrust, Jock accepted the biscuit and
bore it off under the table. Lucca had never had a pet
as a child. He regarded Vivien's dysfunctional dog in
much the same way as he would have regarded any
new project or challenge. But when Jock abandoned
the biscuit to noisily mark Lucca's departure with a
flurry of unimpressed barking, Lucca started laughing.

''You can go back to sleep now…enjoy a lie-in to
recuperate, *cara mia*, 'Lucca teased with the all-male
satisfaction of a guy who had just ravished a woman
within an inch of her life.

Her body indolent after that overdose of pleasure, Vivien lifted languid arms and wound them round his neck. 'Lie-ins are wonderful. Can I assume that you're planning to get Marco up and give him his breakfast?'

Newly aware of the astonishing amount of time and effort that Marco's needs took up at the start of the day, Lucca almost groaned out loud at that question.

A sunny smile of helpless amusement lit up Vivien's face. 'I was only joking...I just wanted to see your reaction!'

'Witch!' Lucca growled with mock annoyance, brilliant golden eyes welded to her lovely laughing face and lingering. At the back of his gaze there was a shadow of concern. Their divorce was final. He had been notified yesterday and he had intended to mention it casually last night. But then he had wondered if she already knew and was preserving a diplomatic silence. He had finally decided that it would be wiser to leave her solicitor to pass on that news. Personalising the announcement might be a mistake, he reasoned. He did not want to upset her.

Conscious of the tension that had tautened his big muscular length, Vivien looked up into his lean bronzed face, heart skipping a beat at his lethal dark attraction. 'What's wrong?'

'Wrong? Nothing.' Shrugging a wide brown shoulder to emphasise that determined negative, Lucca rolled over and sprang out of bed.

So, he was sleeping with his ex-wife! She was happy, Marco was happy and he was happy. Their sleeping arrangements were their own private business. Even so, possibly he should send her some flowers today so that she would know that he appreciated her. Flowers in exchange for a wedding ring, a derisive inner voice enquired. Lucca gritted his teeth.

Perhaps he would also make time to call in at Tiffany's and buy her some diamonds…something spectacular…a necklace or a bracelet. But she wasn't really into jewellery. She would say thank you and put it in a drawer and forget about it again. He would have taken her out to dinner but he didn't want the paparazzi jumping all over them and printing inflammatory stuff in the tabloids that might distress her. He would buy her the most magnificent fern he could find. That would impress, wouldn't it? Something she could stick under a microscope and study if she liked.

'Are you sure there's nothing wrong?' Vivien asked gently, bemused by his most unusual abstraction.

'No, I was just thinking. What we need…what *you* need,' Lucca corrected his phraseology hurriedly and wondered what the hell was wrong with his brain and his usually rock-solid nerves, 'is a nanny to help out with Marco.'

Vivien pretended not to have noticed that slip that revealed that Lucca was once again thinking of them as a couple, but she wanted to grin from ear to ear. 'Rosa Peroli, the nanny who worked part-time for me in Oxford, did say she wouldn't mind trying out city life.'

His brows pleated in surprise. 'Is Rosa Italian?'

Vivien smiled. 'Her parents are and she speaks the language fluently. I thought it was good for Marco to hear Italian spoken in his home as well.'

Lucca was taken aback by that information. Even when the bitterness between them had been at its worst, Vivien had chosen to respect their son's mixed cultural inheritance by employing a nanny of Italian extraction. He had misjudged Vivien. 'She sounds perfect.'

While he was in the shower, Vivien surveyed her untidy bedroom with immense contentment, her green eyes softening with love and sentimental thoughts. Two of Lucca's shirts lay discarded on the floor along with a black tee shirt and a pair of denim jeans that had looked stupendously sexy on him, she reflected dreamily. Three business suits hung from the picture rail. A male hairbrush lay on the dresser beside his mobile. A state of the art little PC, his keys and a file were piled up on the chest of drawers. Various newspapers in Italian and English were scattered throughout the room. He was used to servants, who picked up after him, laundered his linen and dealt with every household task. He really did generate an awful lot of work on the domestic front. And the truth was, the very sight of one of his shirts thrown on the floor made her ecstatically happy.

For two years her bedroom had been a clutter-free zone empty of Lucca and his untidiness and quick-fire energy. She did not even want to think now about how horribly unhappy she had been. After all, why waste time reliving the past when the present was so much better? She had been back in London for only a week and every day Lucca spent more time with her. He was virtually living with her. He was no longer leaving for the office at six in the morning either and he was finishing earlier. The weekend had been wonderful. Incredibly, he had switched off his phone and he had done no work whatsoever. They had had loads of fun with Marco. The simple pleasure of behaving like a family for the very first time was not one she took for granted. She cherished everything they had shared.

Lucca, she was beginning to appreciate, had changed during their time apart. He was so much less arrogant and a lot more unselfish and patient. Time and time again he had demonstrated that he could now temper his own inclinations and compromise for her sake and for Marco's. Yet only two short years ago, Lucca had been very much the kind of male to whom compromise was a dirty word. He had done exactly as he'd wanted when he'd wanted. Her every attempt to make a more secure and comfortable place for herself in his world had ended in abysmal failure.

With hindsight she could now see that, while Lucca might have married her, he had in many ways carried on living his life as though he were still single. She was amazed that she had not registered that reality sooner. She did believe that Lucca had been faithful to her during that year they had first lived together as man and wife, but at the heart of what should have been Lucca's commitment to their life as a couple had been a giant black hole.

He had insisted on hanging onto his flash single-guy apartment even though she'd disliked it. He had refused to moderate his working hours or the frequency of his trips abroad. He had continued to organise his social life without consulting her in any way. They had shared a bed but not much else and what had been shared had been entirely at his discretion. When she had found out that she was pregnant, it had hardly been surprising that she had been unable to picture Lucca adapting to the restrictions that a baby would inflict on his freedom of choice. After all, even though she had been in denial about the fact, Lucca had pretty much refused to make the smallest adaptation to being married.

But in the present that resistance to change had
gone. Lucca was behaving very much like à male keen
to demonstrate how adaptable he could be to family
life. Even when Marco was cranky, Lucca was mar-
vellous with him. On the most personal terms of all,
she reflected in a glow of shy pleasure, Lucca was
being exhaustingly passionate and flatteringly atten-
tive.

Indeed, there was just one cloud on her horizon:
Vivien always liked to know exactly where she stood.
She found it hard to live in an atmosphere of uncertainty and harder still not to question it. If she had had
free choice it would have been to see her future
mapped out in front of her with Lucca locked into a
lifetime contract, but nothing was that simple. It was
true that Lucca was with her at this very moment in
time, but on what terms and for how long? It would
be very dangerous for her to start trying to make assumptions. She felt it was also too soon for her to seek
any form of reassurance. But did they have a future
together again?

Lucca reappeared, superbly dressed in an exquisitely tailored Armani suit. Tall, dark and dazzlingly
handsome, he surveyed her from the foot of the tumbled bed, a charismatic smile curving his beautiful
mouth. He had come up with an innovative solution
to their current situation and he was proud of himself.
'How would you like to take a trip to Italy, *cara*?'

Dragged from her thoughts, Vivien blinked uncertainly. 'Italy?' she echoed in astonishment.

'I have a country house a few miles out of Florence.
We can be private there,' he murmured, thinking how
enchanted she would be when she saw his Tuscan
home. 'We'll leave this afternoon.'

'That soon?' Vivien exclaimed dizzily while wondering when and why he had bought a country house. He had talked about doing that on their honeymoon but nothing had come of it. He had already owned the fabulous villa in Rome, which had been his family home. She had visited it twice in flying visits.

His spectacular dark golden eyes rested on her. 'It would please me a lot, *bella mia*,' he told her.

Rarely had Lucca been so sincere in expressing a sentiment. His beautiful hideaway in the Tuscan hills would be ideal. The paparazzi would not know where they were. Nobody would know where Vivien was either. She was unlikely to receive potentially distressing phone calls from her solicitor or letters. They would both enjoy only perfect peace.

'Then of course I can't wait to go,' Vivien answered softly.

An aspidistra in a magnificent pot was delivered a couple of hours later. She thought it was an unusual gift but rang Lucca and thanked him.

'I know how you feel about ferns, *cara mia*,' he retorted with audible satisfaction.

She thought about telling him that an aspidistra was not a fern, but did not have the heart. He would take it badly. Men never were gracious about mistakes, which they believed entailed a loss of face. In any case it was a very handsome aspidistra.

Bernice phoned mid-morning while Vivien was dragging cases downstairs. Vivien was relieved to hear from her sister and keen to chat and catch up, but soon found herself being subjected to some uncomfortable questioning.

'How long do you have before the divorce becomes final?' Bernice asked baldly.

'I'm not absolutely sure…' Vivien confided, her palms growing damp because she was being forced to think about the very thing she most wished to avoid thinking about.

'Don't be silly. Of course you must know,' Bernice declared, it being quite beyond her to empathise with Vivien's shrinking distaste and fear of the whole procedure of divorce.

Vivien had never wanted a divorce. It was only a couple of months since Lucca, through the usual medium of his legal counsel, had requested a divorce on the grounds of their separation, which had lasted for the required two years. Pride had made her give her consent but she had wept long and hard that night. She had to force herself even to open a letter from her solicitor.

A few weeks earlier, the divorce petition had gone through the court system. The precise date of that event evaded Vivien because she had been too upset to pay much heed to it. However, she was aware that six weeks and a day had to pass before the final decree of divorce could be applied for. She was convinced that that six-week waiting period could not yet have passed and that there was still a small window of opportunity in which Lucca could change his mind and decide that he wanted to stay married.

'Vivien!' Bernice prompted sharply.

'Look…' Vivien was keen to avoid any further discussion of her divorce prospects. Made restive, she tucked the phone between her cheek and her shoulder and went into the porch to lift the small sealed bag of redirected post that had been delivered. It appeared to contain only her favourite seed catalogue and she tossed it into the case she had yet to lock for later perusal. Perhaps it would be more sensible just to be frank with Bernice about what was happening with Lucca, she reflected ruefully. 'Lucca and I are going to Italy this afternoon.'

'Really? I'm delighted for you,' her sister said in a surprisingly bright tone.

Vivien was surprised at Bernice's change of attitude. 'You...*are*?'

'Why shouldn't I be? I have a small confession to make too,' her sister continued in the same bright voice. 'The day you left I mistook your bank statement for mine and accidentally opened it...and I just couldn't help noticing that Lucca has paid the most enormous sum of money into your account.'

Vivien's green eyes rounded. 'My goodness, are you sure?'

'Well, you did ask him for cash and I'll give him his due: he paid up the very same day. Your overdraft has vanished. He's given you two hundred and fifty thousand pounds...a quarter of a mill!' the excited brunette declared.

Astonishment had paralysed Vivien to the spot. 'That much? You're not serious?'

'It's wonderful news for both of us. I can hardly wait for the chance to make a fresh start and now you'll be able to give me an interest-free loan.'

'A loan?' Vivien repeated in bewilderment.

'You're back with Lucca...surely you can spare me a hundred grand to get another business started up?'

At that blunt demand, Vivien breathed in deep. 'But I'm not back with Lucca, not in the way you mean. We could still end up apart,' she confided unhappily. 'I'm really sorry but I couldn't possibly loan you *his* money.'

'Why the hell not? He's rolling in it!' Bernice pointed out in truculent disagreement. 'You *are* sleeping with him again, aren't you?'

Vivien reddened and ignored that intrusive enquiry. 'First and foremost that money was intended to solve my financial problems and ensure Marco's security. I don't have a salary coming in at present. I'm not living in my own home either but I still have the mortgage and bills to meet,' she reminded the brunette uncomfortably. 'The situation I'm in now is temporary—'

'Oh, is it? So, now you're saying you're just Lucca's temporary mistress. Is that right?' her sibling sneered.

That gibe cut Vivien like a knife. 'I really wish that I could help you but at this moment in time—'

'No, you don't...you always were a selfish cow!' Bernice spat in a rage at being refused the loan. 'Lucca's got you right where he wants you. I can't believe it. Three years back, you wouldn't sleep with him until you were engaged—'

'Bernice...please!' Vivien interrupted, stricken with embarrassment.

'And now he only has to stick two hundred grand in your bank account and you're acting like a whore!'

On that abusive note, the phone at the other end of the line was slammed down.

CHAPTER NINE

'YOU'LL love Il Palazzetto,' Lucca forecast with immense confidence.

The name translated as 'the little palace'. Vivien was striving to keep a straight face because she was already picturing crystal chandeliers, vast marble spaces and a lot of gilded finishes. She thought it very unlikely that she would *love* his country house. After all, Lucca liked a great deal of luxury. He had been raised in a sixteenth-century Roman villa with the kind of opulence that made more ordinary people gasp and stare. Too much grandeur made Vivien uncomfortable but she had never expected him to go slumming for her benefit.

It was a glorious day. The limousine was travelling through dense beech woods. Golden sunlight from a perfect blue sky splashed the fresh green leaves and stately pale grey trunks stretched back into the verdant shade created by the closely packed trees.

They turned off the steep road into a winding lane that cut through groves of oak trees that slowly petered out into a lush meadow of poppies and wild flowers. Silhouetted against the backdrop of the wooded hillside, she glimpsed the tall, elegant tower and the terracotta roof of a rambling old house that fitted into the landscape with timeless perfection. Built of warm mellow stone the colour of honey, it looked so impossibly beautiful that her throat ached and her eyes strained to hold that view.

Long before the limo even came to a regal halt on the gravel fronting the ancient building, Vivien was experiencing a deep and disturbing sense of *déjà vu*. Three years ago, they had spent their honeymoon in a contemporary villa filled with cutting-edge technology and furniture that had looked as though it would end up in a design museum. It had been exactly what Lucca liked but she had found the vast echoing spaces soulless and intimidating. On every trip they had enjoyed during that all-too-brief week of being newly marrieds in Tuscany, she had admired the character and beauty of the gracious old houses that she so much preferred. Lucca had started teasing her and he had come up with what he had described as a checklist of her preferences for her dream house.

Her dream home in the Tuscan hill country had been old and stone built. She had also rather fancied a dwelling that rejoiced in a tall handsome tower from which glorious views could be sampled. She had pictured that imaginary house, composite of so many that she had seen, sited on a wooded hillside surrounded by sufficient land to allow total, silent seclusion from the rest of the world. And here it was: her dream house, purchased by her estranged husband for his own use a good month after they had parted. It was enough of a provocation to make even a sane woman scream…

Fortunately for Lucca, Vivien hated screaming at him. Or at least, she hated the aftermath of having screamed when she would feel that such a loss of control reflected badly on her strength of character. Resolving to say nothing about the insulting resemblance Il Palazzetto bore to the fantasy home she had dreamt of while on her honeymoon, Vivien climbed out of the car into the sunlight.

A housekeeper and a maid stepped forward to be introduced and swiftly pounced upon Marco with the kind of enormous appreciation that he most relished. Chuckling at the game the maid initiated, Marco beamed and toddled off happily to receive the cake he had been promised.

'Rosa Peroli will be arriving tomorrow morning to help you look after him,' Lucca informed Vivien.

Blinking rapidly, Vivien stilled and twisted round to look at him. 'Say that again…'

'It wasn't hard to find Rosa's family in the phone book. I called her and asked if she would like to work for you on a full-time basis—'

'But I don't need—'

'It's all organised,' Lucca spelt out. 'Rosa was delighted and said she'd really missed taking care of Marco. She's keen to start work.'

Vivien breathed in so long and so deep in an effort to calm herself that she was fearful she might burst. 'I suppose it didn't occur to you that you should consult me about this arrangement.'

'It did, but I took a considered decision not to consult you.'

Vivien glared at him incredulously. '*Not* to consult me?'

Lucca shrugged wide muscular shoulders sheathed in fine white cotton. 'You're used to being a single parent and if you delegate, you feel guilty. But we should be able to relax together occasionally without worrying about Marco. Taking time just for us isn't a crime, *gioia mia*.'

Sea-green eyes fully lodged to his lean, darkly

handsome features, Vivien stopped glaring and almost smiled for he had employed the cleverest possible words of persuasion. 'I suppose you're right.'

Closing a lean, purposeful hand over hers, he showed her into a big reception room, which contained wonderfully inviting sofas, and had windows that overlooked a welcoming green expanse of garden. All the rooms were well proportioned and furnished with a contemporary take on plain rustic style. Vivien's intense curiosity about who had done the decorating increased rapidly. Il Palazzetto was achingly fashionable. Vivien didn't 'do' trendy interior design but she read the magazines with avid interest. And the deeper she got into Lucca's stunning Tuscan home, the more she found herself imagining Bliss Masterson draping the plaid throw over the wrought-iron seat by the window and adjusting the artfully arranged bare branches that ornamented a starkly simple marble urn. Her chest swelled as she dragged in a quivering breath and struggled to suppress her turbulent emotions. She was trying very hard not to wonder how many other women had enjoyed the same tour with Lucca.

They climbed to the top of the tower to take in the fantastic views of the rolling countryside. In the distance she could see the purplish blue splendour of the mountains. In the haze of the afternoon heat, a medieval village sprawled with higgledy-piggledy charm across a hilltop and looked for all the world as though it belonged in a children's fairy tale. Dense woods, silvery green olive groves and flourishing vineyards adorned a lush green landscape of breathtaking beauty.

But Vivien was not properly appreciative. Indeed her eyes burned with pent-up tears and the images were blurring. She was still picturing Bliss twitching those branches into stylish harmony with her thin, elegant fingers. She had sworn to herself that she would say nothing but the torments of her own imagination were more than flesh and blood could stand. 'You know…you promised me a house exactly like this on our honeymoon.'

'I always deliver,' Lucca drawled teasingly.

Vivien went so tense she was surprised her bones didn't crack. How could he be so obtuse? Did he think she had been complimenting him? The exploration continued. She preceded him into a bedroom where pale blue drapes fell to a polished oak floor. Soft blue, her favourite colour. Her delicate face tightened. Like a police detective hot on the scent of a dangerous criminal, she pushed open the door into what she deemed to be the *en suite* and there it was, the final proof of his gross insensitivity: the free-standing, exquisitely shaped bath of her dreams!

'I hate you!' Vivien launched at Lucca on the back of an angry sob.

Lean, powerful face impassive, Lucca backed up against the footboard of the impressive wooden bed and studied her in apparent astonishment. '*Santo Cielo*… I don't believe I'm hearing this. What's the matter with you?'

'You bought my dream home after I'd left you and desecrated it with other women!' Vivien screeched at him. 'How dare you bring me here?'

'Possibly I wanted to remind you of what a great guy you walked out on, *bella mia*,' Lucca countered with ice cool clarity. 'What you're seeing here isn't what you think it is…what you're seeing here within these four walls is the faith I once had in you.'

'What's that supposed to mean?' she slung back shakily.

'I thought you'd come back to me. It did not once occur to me when you packed and left our home that that would be the end of our marriage.'

Shimmering dark golden eyes seared her strained face.

'A week after you walked out, I was given the details of this place. Prior to that, I'd rejected the offer of several properties,' Lucca confided coldly. 'I knew the minute I saw the photos that Il Palazzetto was your fantasy house and fantasies don't come on the market every week. I bought it because I sincerely believed that you would soon come to your senses and be living with me as my wife again.'

A hard lump had formed in Vivien's throat, for she had been totally unprepared for an explanation that knocked her sideways. As he gazed back at her in hard male challenge, the warm colour in her cheeks ebbed. 'If that's true—'

His gorgeous golden eyes hardened. 'Don't doubt my word. You did that once with devastating consequences,' he reminded her drily. 'I would think you would have learned a lesson on that score.'

In the uneasy silence, an unsteady laugh fell from Vivien's lips. 'Yes, I have learned a lesson or two. I misjudged you but I would have been very willing to be persuaded into crediting the truth of your fidelity, had you ever given me the chance. You didn't care enough about me to come after me and fight to get me back!'

His wide, sensual mouth firmed. 'That's a lie.'

'You were too proud. I hurt your ego by not believing in you and you decided to punish me,' Vivien told him with bitter pain in her voice.

'That's a very fanciful view of events.'

'No, it's very much you,' Vivien contradicted tightly. 'You were playing Russian roulette with our marriage. Now I know the whole story because you've told me it. You bought this house only because you were expecting me to come back and grovel.'

'Your imagination is taking flight again,' Lucca derided, assuming a maddeningly cool attitude of relaxation.

'You were cruel to both of us. You were so angry with me for not grovelling that you let me go. But you can just stop right now blaming me for the breakdown of our marriage. I may not have been a perfect wife but you were an even worse husband. You made me miserable long before Jasmine Bailey got her poison pen out!'

A slight rise of dark blood demarcated Lucca's hard angular cheekbones and his dark golden eyes flashed. 'On what facts do you base that accusation?'

'Our marriage fell apart because I never saw you. You put business first and, every excuse you got, you made me feel just how unimportant I was in your scheme of things. You didn't really want to be married. You acted like you were still single—'

'*Per meraviglia!* Is it my fault you were a doormat and took everything I dished out? What's the point of complaining about how I treated you two years too late?' Lucca suddenly raked across the room at her, full volume. 'I was twenty-seven years old when we got married and not as mature as I thought I was. I didn't really know *how* to be married.'

'I didn't realise you needed a rule book!'

His strong jaw line squared. 'Maybe you didn't, but I would have found one helpful. My own parents lived separate lives. My father had continual affairs and my mother had a long-term lover. They loathed each other,' he admitted curtly. 'It was quite astonishing that they died in the same plane crash because they rarely went anywhere together.'

Vivien was silenced, absolutely silenced by that explanation. His parents had died before she'd even met him and it had never once occurred to her that his family background might have been unhappy. 'Serafina never even hinted...'

'Serafina was still a child when they died and I saw no reason to disillusion her.'

'But you should have told me.'

His arrogant dark head lifted high, beautiful dark golden eyes gleaming with stubborn disagreement. 'Why? It has no bearing on what happened between us. I only pointed out that my parents' marriage didn't give me a constructive blueprint for the kind of cosy blanket domesticity you wanted.'

Big words from a guy who had been revelling in cosy blanket domesticity all week long! But thanks to what he had finally got angry enough to reveal, she was now able to view the extent of his wary cynicism and reserve when they were first married in a very different light. With his history, she marvelled that he had ever proposed to her. She lifted her chin. 'Did you really buy this house for me?'

Lucca slung her a stony glance.

All of a sudden, Vivien was starting to feel very much more confident. 'Yeah, you really did buy it for me,' she answered for herself, relishing that ego-boosting truth. 'Rustic is not exactly you, is it?'

A flare of gold highlighted the long-lashed brilliance of his eyes. 'There are some rural pleasures I can appreciate, *bella mia.*'

Vivien had a startlingly vivid recollection of being tumbled down in long grass and possessed with a sexual fervour she still remembered three years after the event. Lucca strolled lazily forward with soundless grace. His gorgeous eyes never left hers once. He let her see his hunger.

Desire leapt into the atmosphere and she felt hot and tight and needy. She trembled, a wicked frisson of instant excitement quivering through her. Her mouth running dry, she kicked off her shoes. He looked surprised and then he backed to the door to force it shut. He strode back. 'I used to imagine you here in this room.'

Satisfaction assailed her in a heady burst. She felt irresistible. Unfastening the zip on her dress, she hauled it off in one feverish motion.

'Keep going...' Lucca instructed thickly.

She unhooked her bra. He couldn't take his eyes off her. She arched her spine and let the scrap of lace fall.

'Don't stop there...' Lucca urged huskily.

She stepped out of her last garment. Her face was hot with self-consciousness and a nervous giggle escaped her as she arranged herself on the big wide bed. 'So come here,' she told him, half under her breath.

Lucca ripped off his shirt and sent a couple of buttons flying. Slim and pale and a magnet for his mesmerised attention, she stretched, enjoying the shafts of sunlight warming her skin and revelling in his interest.

He was fascinated. 'When did you get to be so shameless?'

'After a week of you,' she whispered daringly, and she felt wild and brazen and she loved the sensation.

'I've never brought another woman here,' Lucca confessed, shedding his jeans. 'I came here for peace and solitude.'

It was *her* place. She should have known it in her bones, she thought happily. He scored an appreciative hand over the silken swell of her small, full breasts and lowered his head to taste a lush rosy crest. A short, sharp gasp parted her lips and her fingers speared into his black hair as her tender flesh peaked into rigid response. He put his mouth there and she was lost.

Every nerve ending she possessed tingled and she trembled, wildly aware of the moist, tight sensitivity between her thighs. She shifted beneath him, squirmed, hauled him down to her, craving what only he could give and too hungry to hide it. He looked down into her passion-glazed eyes. 'I want you so much I ache…' he told her raggedly.

'What are you waiting for?' she whispered back, staring up at him, adoring every sleek, hard, masculine line of his bronzed features and most of all the stunning golden eyes welded to her. 'I'm yours.'

'You weren't when you walked away—'

'If I can forgive you…you can forgive me,' she breathed, holding his intense gaze with her own. 'I'm back and I'm staying.'

He seized on that encouragement with a passion and a level of fierce hunger that blew her away. Afterwards he sprawled back against the tumbled pillows, all-conquering hero and momentarily replete. Shell-shocked by the amount of pleasure he had given her and just a little mortified by the intensity of her own response, she let him rearrange her limp and satiated body on top of him.

'How was I?' he said wickedly.

She breathed in the intoxicating scent of his damp skin and smiled to herself before mumbling, 'You need lots and lots of practice.'

Lean fingers tipped up her chin and she went off into helpless giggles. He rolled her under him and held her fast. 'Was that a complaint, *bella mia*?'

'Marco will think we've got lost,' she said guiltily. 'We'd better get up before he misses us.'

Lucca headed into the shower. Her body deliciously relaxed and heavy, she could easily have fallen asleep. When the phone by the bed began ringing, she groaned and reached out and answered it.

For a moment silence buzzed on the line.

'Vivien? Is that you? Is that *really* you?' a familiar female voice exclaimed on an excited high. 'I couldn't believe it when I heard you speak!'

It was Lucca's sister, Serafina, and Vivien sat up with a start, suddenly fully awake and aware.

'Oh, my gosh…oh, my gosh, you're with Lucca at Il Palazzetto! You and my brother are back together again. That means you'll be at my wedding on Saturday. This is the best gift I could ever have!' the bubbly brunette proclaimed chokily. 'Were the two of you just going to turn up together without telling me?'

'Let me get Lucca…' Vivien dropped the receiver as though it had burned her. She really did not know what to say to Serafina, to whom she had grown very close during her marriage. But when Vivien had left Lucca, Serafina had spoken up with spirit in her brother's defence. Looking back, Vivien could have wept for her own refusal to listen. It had seemed eas-

iest back then to let her contact with the younger
woman die.

Vivien called Lucca to the phone and tried not to
feel hurt about the fact that he had not even told her
that his sister was engaged and about to get married.
Had he been planning to take her to Serafina's wedding? It would be difficult for him to do otherwise
now.

A towel knotted round his lean hips and crystalline
drops of water still beading his hair-roughened chest,
Lucca swept up the phone and Vivien left him to
freshen up and get dressed as fast as she could.

'Serafina is planning a night out on the town with
her friends tomorrow evening and she wants you to
join them,' Lucca volunteered with a grimace when
she reappeared in the bedroom. He was still on the
phone. 'I'm trying to tell her that that kind of thing
just isn't your style.'

The rebel inside Vivien rose up. She assumed that
he preferred to keep his sister and her apart and she
saw no reason why she should play along. 'You're
wrong…I'd love to go, and thank her for asking me.'

Lucca looked startled and disapproving.

Vivien felt like a ninety-two-year-old who had confessed to a desire to go clubbing with teenagers. But
Serafina was only four years her junior. He passed the
phone back to her. His sister chattered on at an in-
credible rate of knots, confided that she couldn't wait
to see Vivien again and finally rang off.

'To whom is she getting married?' Vivien enquired
rather stiltedly then.

His lean, strong face was taut. 'Umberto, he's an
architect…and he's besotted with her.'

Vivien dropped her head. 'I'm happy for her. Did

you tell her how things were with us?' she asked, fishing and shockingly grateful for the excuse to do so. 'She was really jumping to conclusions.'

'That's my sister. Let her think what she likes until after the wedding,' Lucca advised without any expression at all.

'Are you planning on taking me to her wedding?'

'I don't think we have much choice now that she knows you're here in Italy.'

It was not the most generous reply and it made Vivien suspect that, but for Serafina's intervention, Lucca would not have dreamt of taking her to a family wedding. After all, Vivien was well aware that her appearance at such an event would cause a sensation amongst his friends and relatives. At the same time, in answering Vivien in such an evasive way, Lucca had resisted the opportunity to define what they were sharing. She felt rather cut off and very much regretted having answered that phone call. Although, perhaps, she reasoned, she was being oversensitive. Perhaps it was too soon for Lucca to feel up to talking about their new relationship.

A hundred years from now, he wouldn't feel up to talking about it, Vivien acknowledged rucfully. Expecting him to start talking about relationships was wishing for the moon. He was never stuck for a ready word when it came to any other subject. But a question that related to emotions was capable of clearing him from the room. A question that related to both emotions and commitment might well be capable of chasing him from the house. Lucca was, after all, the guy who had set up the romantic proposal scene at Longchamp complete with champagne, strawberries and diamond ring and then just said, 'Well…will you?'

'Will I what?' she asked, surveying the diamonds sparkling in the sunlight with prayer and heady hope in her heart.

Seething with obvious frustration, he dealt her a look of fierce reproach. Lifting her hand, he slotted the engagement ring onto her finger. 'So…you and I?'

'Is this marriage we're not talking about?' Vivien whispered.

'The engagement comes first,' Lucca hastened to assert.

'But marriage is the target?'

Without any warning at all, a wicked grin chased the tension from his beautiful mouth. '*Sì, amata mia.* Marriage is the target.'

He had called her 'my love' and that had been the closest he had ever come to a declaration of love. She had loved him too much to put pressure on him. She had thought that his inability to talk about really important feelings was a sign of just how deep his feelings ran and she had been touched and she had felt ridiculously protective towards him. But, with hindsight, she could see that she should have put a contract down in front of him and the negotiations would have resulted in agreed conditions. That way, there would have been no misunderstandings. That way they would both have known what they'd been getting into and he would have enjoyed fighting to get the best deal he could.

The following morning, Lucca had a meeting with his farm manager. Their nanny, Rosa Peroli, was due to arrive and Vivien took Marco out onto the shaded terrace beyond the salon and sat down to enjoy a cup of coffee and her favourite seed catalogue. It was only when she removed the plastic redirection bag from the catalogue that she realised that what she had assumed to be the envelope included for a potential order was actually a separate letter. And a communication from her solicitor, no less. A chilled sensation locked her tummy muscles tight.

The letter was short and to the point. Having tried and failed to contact her at home by phone during the earlier part of the week, her solicitor was writing to inform her that her divorce was now final. The coffee in her mouth turned to acid. She raised stricken eyes as Marco squealed with delight over the noisy plastic-shape-sorter toy that he was playing with.

Her thoughts flailed around in a cruel circle of jagged reaction. She was divorced. She was no longer married to Lucca. She was not Lucca's wife any more and he was not her husband any more either. She felt sick with shock and then sick and angry at her own inadequacy. Why hadn't she called her solicitor to find out exactly where their divorce was on the time line? Where had that avoidance got her now? What sort of madness had it been to bury her head in the sand and hope that there would still be time for a last-ditch miracle?

Lucca had warned her, though, hadn't he? Our marriage is over, he had said, and predictably he had been right. He had to know that they were now divorced. With a trembling hand she snatched up the letter she had allowed to fall at her feet and scrutinised the date. According to her estimate, Lucca had to have known for a few days at least.

He hadn't said a word either. Not a single word. Of course, what else would she have expected? Lucca

Saracino was far too clever to be the guy who broke
bad news of that nature. Of course, it was possible that
he thought she already knew and was taking his lead
from her in not mentioning it. No, she was being too
generous, she decided in an agony of pain and regret.
Lucca *knew*. He knew very well when to keep quiet
too.

A burning gush of tears hit her eyes and she blinked
rapidly and snatched in a quivering breath. Well, her
fairy-tale happy ending had been ripped apart,
squashed flat and then dumped. Who liked facing hurtful things? That she was divorced surely gave her the
answers she had sought over the past ten days. He
might be willing to sleep with her, but he had let their
divorce go through. He had made no attempt to save
their marriage because he had not valued what remained of it as she did. It was obvious that what she
had naively thought they had recaptured was a figment
of her own stupid imagination.

Her thoughts leapt to the immediate future and the
necessity of giving Lucca the widest possible berth
until she had got herself back under control and decided what to do next. As soon as Rosa arrived, they
were leaving for Rome to enable Vivien to go out with
Serafina and her friends that evening. When they got
to Rome, she would insist that she needed to go and
buy something to wear. A shopping trip would grant
her the space she needed. What was she planning on
doing? Was she going to weather this storm and stay?
Or claim defeat and leave?

Marco laughed out loud. With an effort, Vivien recalled her son and peered round the chair to check on
him. He had trailed out the contents of her handbag
and he was drawing on his face with a lipstick. She

got up on legs that felt like jelly and took it off him before he started eating it. Deprived of the bag as well, her son loosed a plaintive howl of complaint.

'*Dio mio…*' Lucca's honeyed drawl interposed as he strolled along the terrace and picked up the little boy. 'What a racket, Marco.'

Vivien dug the solicitor's letter into her bag. She just wanted to run away but knew she could not. She was fiercely glad that she had not let the tears take hold. The only thing she had left was her pride and could she even claim that? Why had he brought her out to Italy?

Maybe he had thought he had to sleep with her to gain better access to Marco, she thought feverishly as she pretended to be looking for something in her bag. Maybe he was on a revenge trip and hooked on the buzz of punishing her for daring to leave him in the first place. Maybe he truly did like sex with her so much that he was quite content to let that be the extent of their relationship. And she had agreed? If he'd suggested a mission to Mars with sex thrown in, she would have agreed, wouldn't she? Was it fair to blame him for the fact that she had been *so* easy?

'I thinks Marco needs to be washed,' Lucca pointed out, wondering whether she was annoyed because his meeting had dragged on longer than he had originally forecast.

Vivien focused on Marco, who had spread her peach lipstick all over his face and his father's shirt and who was now being held at arm's length like a source of dangerous contamination. Her throat was so choked with tears she could not speak. She did not know whether she was angrier with Lucca or with herself. But beyond the anger lurked a great horrible well of humiliation. She had chased him in time-honoured style and got her just deserts, it seemed. She was exceedingly grateful when the housekeeper chose that moment to show Rosa Peroli out to the terrace.

Vivien chattered relentlessly all the way to Rome and thought she had done a remarkable job of concealing her emotional devastation.

'What's wrong?' Lucca demanded the instant they arrived at the family villa and Rosa had been installed in the nursery suite with their son.

'Nothing…why should there be anything wrong?'

'I just know there is,' Lucca countered squarely, dark golden eyes striving to read her pale delicate face and shuttered gaze. 'Why do you want to go out alone this afternoon? You hate shopping.'

'Not always.'

Lucca reached for her hand. It lay in his like a hand carved in ice. 'I would like to come with you.'

'You can't. I might decide to get my hair done,' she protested.

When Lucca had left the room, Vivien removed her wedding ring and set it down on an elegant chest of drawers. The ring had been a symbol of their marriage and she no longer wanted to wear it. She hoped he did not think that she was making some kind of cheap point. But she knew that she had to rethink their relationship as it now was. At best she was having an affair with her ex-husband. At worst, she was likely to be labelled his mistress. Something rather less respectable than being a wife and decidedly less safe in terms of commitment. Her choice was to accept that or reject it. Right at that moment she reckoned that she hated Lucca as much as she loved him.

It was the very best possible time for Serafina to

knock on the bedroom door and hurry in with a delighted smile. A slim young woman with warm brown
eyes and a torrent of black curls, she gave Vivien an
excited hug. 'We are going to have a wild time tonight,' she swore. 'But don't feel the need to tell
Lucca...he still treats me like I'm a child!'

CHAPTER TEN

'NO WAY should you be going out dressed like that!'

As if Lucca had not spoken, Vivien added another layer of mascara to her lashes. What she wore was really none of his business. She had gone shopping with Serafina, who had been terrific company and exactly the distraction she needed from her unhappy thoughts. Serafina had persuaded her to buy a short cream leather skirt, a very flattering pale green fitted top and a pair of knee-high soft suede boots.

'It's a very sexy outfit…OK,' Lucca conceded, striving to hang onto his temper, which was difficult when he was in the act of working out that about sixty-five per cent of Vivien's fabulous figure and stunning legs were on show. 'Wear that kind of stuff for me but don't go *out* in it. It's not appropriate.'

'You think I'm too old and staid for a skirt that shows my knees?' Vivien asked in a tight little voice.

'No, but it will attract the sort of attention you dislike. Other men are likely to come on to you,' Lucca delivered, wondering what the hell had come over her for about the hundredth time since they had left Il Palazzetto. All the way to Rome she had talked to their nanny, Rosa, and to Marco but had continually left him out in the cold. She looked at him and yet somehow managed never to meet his eyes direct.

It was only at that point that his attention fell on the wedding ring lying on the chest of drawers beside him and whipped straight to her newly bare left hand.

For a split second, he felt as if he had been punched in the gut and flung over a cliff.

'You're not wearing your wedding ring,' Lucca breathed flatly.

'Now that we're divorced, I don't think I should.' Vivien was proud of the level voice that emerged from her dry mouth.

'I'm very shocked that, you would take it off, *cara mia*,' Lucca confided with sincerity, striving not to react to the news that she had finally discovered that they were divorced. He concentrated on the ring issue, which he realised had quite overpowering significance for him. 'I think you should keep your ring on.'

'No, it's part of the past and I'm not your wife any more. I just wouldn't feel comfortable wearing it now.'

A silence screaming with undertones fell. She kept on adding more mascara to her lashes and was vaguely surprised that they didn't fall off under the weight. She lifted a lipstick.

'When did you realise that the divorce had gone through?' Lucca asked abruptly.

She explained and added, 'You must have guessed I didn't know...I wish you'd told me.'

Lucca sought to excuse the inexcusable. 'It didn't seem important.'

Her teeth gritted on the angry words of distress that threatened to pour from her in spirited disagreement. Their marriage had been extremely important to her.

Aware that what he had just said had come out wrong, Lucca regrouped and murmured urgently, 'What I meant to say is...what's important is that we're together. We're very much together—'

'And divorced,' Vivien slotted in helplessly.

'We're happier than we were when we were first married.' His lean powerful face was taut, dark golden eyes intent. 'We know what went wrong and we don't need a marriage licence to tell us that what we have is worth keeping.'

Involuntarily, Vivien was impressed. At least his words proved that he valued their relationship and that he did see a future for them. But inside herself she still felt savaged by the knowledge that they were no longer man and wife.

Lucca extended her wedding ring. 'Please put it back on.'

'I said no,' she reminded him tightly and resisted the urge to tell him that if he wanted her to wear a wedding ring he shouldn't have divorced her.

His lean dark features clenched. 'People are likely to think you're single.'

'I am.'

'*Dannazione*...what the hell is that supposed to mean?' Lucca growled with sudden aggression.

Vivien gave him a frowning appraisal.

'And what's with all the make-up?' Lucca's famed self-discipline slipped another notch. 'You rarely even use lipstick but here you are tonight painting yourself from head to toe! Any guy would be forgiven for wondering if you were going out on the pull!'

'With your sister in tow, I think that's unlikely.' Vivien rose from the dressing stool and hid a smile. Maybe he had expected her to dress all in black and sob in the corner on the day she learned that they were divorced. Well, she was grateful to have disappointed his expectations and if he thought that she was in the mood to party, even better.

As the limo door closed on Vivien and Serafina, the

younger woman grinned and shook her head in apparent wonderment. 'Lucca's so incredibly possessive of you…it's sweet. I used to have this very cool image of my brother but he's in a cold sweat just because you're looking gorgeous and going clubbing without him!'

Vivien's smile grew a little less forced and her eyes warmed. 'You think so?'

'I never thought I'd see the day but I think so. Umberto had invited Lucca to join his friends tonight but Lucca turned him down. But I bet you anything that Lucca goes now. The men are supposed to be meeting up with us at midnight.'

Seated in a dark corner, Vivien saw Lucca the instant he entered the club.

He was with a group but she saw only him. His height was distinctive. A down light gleamed over his arrogant dark head and gilded his strong cheekbones. Her heart skipped a beat and she breathed in deep. She was planning to play it very cool but she was really relieved that he had decided to come.

She had spent the evening smiling until her jaw ached and avoiding male advances. Men had continually approached her. Serafina and her friends were split in their opinion of whether it was the leather skirt or the high-heeled boots that was the main attraction. But Vivien knew she should have listened to Lucca. While she had thought it would be nice to be admired, men cornering her to chat her up put her in just as big a panic now as they had done when she was a teenager.

She had thought over what Lucca had said and she felt a lot calmer and a little less hurt and rejected. To be fair to him, it had been a bit late in the day to call off their divorce. She had to be realistic: it *was* only ten days since they had got back together. He was right too in that they were more together than they had ever been. Without a doubt, she understood him an awful lot better and probably loved him a great deal more. Losing him once had scarred her but it had also, she had finally grasped, made her stronger and more independent. So, what was in a wedding ring? No magic answer, she decided, determined to keep up her spirits.

Lucca sank down behind the table and tugged her towards him. His stunning dark golden eyes locked to hers. Either she moved or he moved or they both moved simultaneously. Whatever, he closed his hands into her hair to hold her entrapped and took her mouth with a passionate urgency that lit her up inside like a bonfire.

'Lucca…' she said breathlessly, subsiding against him.

A satisfied smile chased the tension from his wide sensual lips. 'We'll get married again as soon as it can be arranged.'

In total disconcertion, Vivien studied him. 'Why?'

'You're happier being married, *bella mia*,' Lucca murmured smoothly. 'I want you to be happy.'

He might as well have prodded her with a hot toasting fork. She pushed herself back from him. She was horribly tempted to slap him but was unsure that she would be able to stop at just one slap. As proposals went it was a killer, for it both patronised and humiliated. How dared he?

'Of course, it will make me happy too,' Lucca added belatedly.

'Then you've got a problem because I don't want to marry you again. Once was quite sufficient.'

'You want me to get down on my knees in a public place?' Lucca raked at her in a raw undertone.

She almost said yes just to see him explode. She was furious with him. 'Which part of the word no don't you understand?'

'You're driving me crazy…' Lucca groaned, scorching golden eyes welded to her lovely face.

'Let me tell you something…I'm quite happy being single—'

'You weren't happy about it this afternoon,' Lucca interposed very drily. 'So what's changed? Has some toy boy caught your eye?'

'It would serve you right if one had!' Her sea-green eyes flashed at him, her temper fully alight.

'I'd kill him…if another man touched you, I'd tear him apart with my bare hands!' Lucca swore explosively. 'Stop playing games with me. Why don't you want to marry me?'

'I'll only marry for love …and you don't love me.'

Raw frustration blazed in his brilliant gaze. He grabbed both her hands to hold her because she was backing away. 'Vivi…'

The silence pulsed and roared. She waited. He compressed his stubborn mouth. She thrust him back from her in angry rejection. 'Leave me alone!'

In the midst of that high-voltage moment, a guy leant over the table to say to her, 'Can I buy you a drink?'

'She's with me!' Lucca told him curtly.

'I saw her push you away…is he annoying you?' the stranger turned to ask Vivien.

'Stay out of this,' Lucca warned with a lethal quietness that made the nape of Vivien's neck prickle.

Vivien could see a situation developing and she scrambled up to head for the cloakroom, believing that that would give Lucca the chance to calm down. But Lucca moved faster than she did. Before she could step out from behind the table, Lucca had swung a punch at the stranger. As she cried out in horror a fight broke out with a speed and violence that appalled her.

It was amazing how many men flung themselves with frightening enthusiasm into that free-for-all of a fight. While Vivien and Serafina looked on in disbelief from a safe distance, the police arrested Lucca and several other men.

'My brother is never going to live this down.' Serafina laughed because nobody had really been hurt, but Vivien was still horrified.

She blamed herself. Lucca had proposed and it had been a clumsy proposal but nobody knew better than her that he was dismal at proposing. She had said no when he'd least expected it. He was very confident and he had not been mentally prepared for that negative response. How he had gone off the deep end into that fight she did not quite comprehend, but she believed that it was her fault that he had lost control. He had never, ever done anything like that before. She felt that she should have recognised that, though Lucca might be better at hiding it than she was, he had been under a lot of stress too.

Lucca was not released by the police until the next morning. No charges were laid against him. The paparazzi had photographed him leaving the nightclub in police custody and the picture made headlines in the gossip columns. 'Saracino fights over ex-wife.'

When the drawing-room door opened, Vivien glanced up, expecting it to be Lucca. She was astonished to see her sister instead. 'Bernice?'

'Are you still angry with me? I was scared to phone ahead,' Bernice pulled an anxious face. 'I thought you might refuse to see me because I was so rude the last time we spoke.'

Vivien stood up to welcome her with a smile. 'I wouldn't behave like that. You're my sister,' she reminded her quietly. 'How did you find out where I was staying?'

'I guessed. Lucca threw your engagement party here…don't you remember?'

Vivien had forgotten and, recalling how nervous and awkward she had been that evening, she smiled more naturally. 'What on earth has brought you all the way to Italy?'

As she took a seat Bernice lowered her pale blue eyes. 'There's something I have to tell you. I probably should have told you years ago but I didn't want to hurt you. However, now that you've gone back to Lucca, I feel it's my duty to speak up.'

Listening, Vivien became very tense. 'I have no idea what you're talking about.'

'I was really shocked to find out that Lucca had been arrested for violence,' her sister added with a satisfaction she could not conceal. 'It's in all the newspapers.'

'That was a misunderstanding…' Vivien looked across the room because Lucca had appeared in the doorway. He gave her a smile that turned her heart upside down and held his finger to his mouth to let her know that he didn't want her to mention his presence to Bernice.

'I wouldn't be too sure. He might be thumping you next—'

'I really don't think so,' Vivien said hastily, watching Lucca freeze in the act of walking away and then swinging back at decisive speed. After that comment from Bernice, she felt she could hardly blame him for choosing to stay around. 'Let's not talk about this.'

'You know I don't like Lucca. Didn't you ever wonder why?' Bernice probed as if Vivien hadn't spoken. 'Well, it's quite simple. A couple of months after you got married, Lucca made a *very* heavy pass at me.'

Vivien could feel her own face tighten like concrete setting and she could not bring herself to glance in Lucca's direction. 'Why have you waited so long to tell me this?'

'There was no need to tell you when you were getting divorced. But now you're back living with him.'

'How much cash are you hoping to make from that allegation, Bernice?' Lucca asked, cool as a mountain spring.

Visibly dismayed by that interruption, Bernice flushed to the roots of her hair and sprang upright as Lucca strolled into view. 'What are you trying to imply?'

'That greed for money has to be connected in some way to this dramatic tale,' Lucca contended levelly. 'I can't let this go. I'm going to have to tell Vivien about some of the other things you've done—'

'Don't you dare tell Vivien lies about me!' Bernice hissed at him.

Lucca dealt her a sardonic appraisal. 'I can prove everything I have to say. If I kept quiet until now, it was only to protect Vivien. But when you attempt to threaten us, you have to be stopped,' he murmured

grimly, and he turned his keen dark gaze on Vivien.
'Bernice took your late father for everything he had.
He had paid her debts several times over by the time
he died. As soon as we were married, she approached
me for money.'

'That's not true…' the brunette condemned.

'Her boutique was in trouble once again and she
needed a loan,' Lucca explained. 'I knew she was a
very poor financial risk but she was your sibling and
you were fond of her. A loan was extended to her. As
I had expected, it wasn't repaid and I felt I'd done as
much as I could do for a member of your family—'

'He's talking rubbish,' Bernice interrupted, focusing
pleading eyes on her silent sister. 'You can't trust a
word he says. Don't you know that yet?'

'I understand now why you were so eager to keep
Lucca and I apart.' Vivien sighed heavily, for she was
very hurt that her sister should have plotted and
planned and lied solely in an effort to enrich herself
at her expense. 'If we reconciled, you were very unlikely to gain access to more money. You knew Lucca
would tell me the truth if he found out that you were
trying to persuade me into giving you a loan.'

'Why aren't you listening to my side of the story?'
Bernice shouted at Vivien, incredulous at the reception
she was receiving. 'Why won't you believe me?'

Vivien winced. 'Because you've always told lies,'
she responded reluctantly. 'Quite blatant lies too.
Lucca, on the other hand, tells the truth and shames
the devil!'

'You deserve a smart ass like him!' Bernice flung
in raging mortification and she flounced out of
the room.

'Yes. I think I finally do,' Vivien agreed and she finally let herself glance at Lucca.

Lucca appeared to be in a rare state of shock and riveted to the spot.

'Give me five minutes,' she begged and hurried off in Bernice's wake.

Her sister was standing in the hall in floods of tears.

'Stay the night here,' Vivien proffered gently. 'I don't want you rushing off when you're feeling like this.'

'I can't stand you being nice to me after what I've just tried to do!' Bernice gasped. 'You should hate me!'

'You're my sister and you're unhappy. That's all that really matters.'

But Bernice could not face the prospect of seeing Lucca again and insisted on leaving. She planned to head straight back to the airport. Vivien made her promise to keep in touch.

Lucca watched Vivien walk back into the room and released his breath in a slow hiss. 'You were amazing, *cara mia*. I was so scared you might listen to her.'

'I knew the minute Bernice arrived that she was up to something because she was putting on such an act.' Vivien grimaced. 'You should have told me about the loan you'd given her. It would have been better for her if she had had to take some responsibility for failing to repay that money. Instead she went on to get herself into more debt.'

'She is addicted to spending money she doesn't have. She needs professional support to sort her out. But must we talk about your sister's problems now?'

Vivien went pink. 'No…'

'Can you forgive me for the way I behaved last night?' Lucca asked her then.

'You're a caveman under those Armani suits. I had no idea.'

Colour marked his strong cheekbones and he winced. 'When you stood up, I thought you were about to go off and have a drink with that guy. That's why I hit him.'

'I wouldn't have done something like that!'

'When you said you wouldn't marry me, it was like the roof fell in. I'd had a few drinks. I was jealous…'

Vivien studied him with wide-eyed fascination. 'Why are you telling me all this?'

'I don't want to lose you again,' Lucca confessed roughly, his accent very thick.

'Would that matter so much?' she whispered.

He vented a rueful laugh. 'How can you ask me that? All I have ever really cared about is you. Possibly you think I have a strange way of showing that but in my own defence…I didn't know how much you meant to me until you walked out two years ago.'

Vivien was very still, almost afraid to move in case she spooked him into silence. 'How did you feel?'

'Like death for months and months and months, *bella mia.*' Lucca raked a not quite steady hand through his cropped black hair and fixed strained dark golden eyes on her. 'It was about a year until there was another woman and I had to pretend she was you…'

That gruff, low-pitched admission petered out with a look of pain and forced her to wrinkle her nose to will the hot tears back. 'So, why didn't you come and see me?'

'You were right about my pride. I believed you'd

come back to me. When you didn't, you showed yourself to be strong. But once you'd demonstrated that, how could I be weak enough to chase after you?' Lucca asked heavily, watching enlightenment cross her face closely followed by appalled regret. 'I wouldn't admit how miserable I was even to myself.'

'I couldn't bear to be that miserable ever again,' Vivien confided chokily. 'It was the worst pain ever.'

'So when you showed up in my office I was being torn in a dozen opposing directions. I wanted you and I didn't want you. I didn't want to be hurt again either,' he confessed with obvious difficulty. 'I believed I wanted to punish you and then slowly it started to occur to me that that wasn't really what I was trying to do…'

'It…*wasn't*?' Vivien was getting lost in his explanation.

'I let the divorce go through because I needed to see that you would stay with me even if we weren't married. I was testing you out like a stupid kid…I wanted you to prove that you loved me—'

Her swimming eyes overflowed. 'I wanted you to prove the same thing…so that's OK.'

Troubled dark golden eyes assailed hers. 'I don't know *how* to prove I love you.'

She thought of the fight he had started in the club the night before. She thought of the fear he had betrayed just minutes earlier. She thought of the natural bravado behind which he hid his human moments of uncertainty. And lastly, she thought of the way he was sacrificing his cool front and forcing himself to talk because he was afraid of losing her. She flung herself into his arms and held him tight. 'Just tell me and I'll believe you.'

'I love you, *amata mia*.'

A cocoon of blissful happiness enclosed her. 'I love you too. Will you marry me?'

Lucca tensed. 'I thought that was my line.'

Vivien was amused. 'But you're not that hot at it, so I thought it would be easier if I took care of it. Well, will you or won't you?'

'I will.'

'OK …now there are one or two little conditions,' Vivien added winsomely.

'Conditions?'

'Nothing too onerous…just shorter working hours, only occasional foreign trips, another two children—'

'Lots and lots of sex.' Lucca was getting into the spirit of the occasion. 'You never, ever take your wedding ring off. So when do we get married again?'

'As soon as you like,' Vivien told him blissfully, certain that this time around they would get everything right.

A year later, Vivien became the mother of a baby girl called Pia.

Eleven months earlier, Lucca and Vivien had remarried in a quiet London ceremony with the already-married Serafina and Umberto acting as their witnesses. For a long time after that life had literally been one long glorious honeymoon for Lucca and Vivien. With Marco young enough to travel freely, his parents had flitted between Italy and England according to their mood. They had been entirely self-indulgent.

Lucca had set up an office in Florence and built an experimental fernery for Vivien in a special glasshouse at Il Palazzetto. While she'd been pregnant with Pia she'd written a very entertaining book about the his-

tory of fern exploration, which had sold well to bot-
anists. Bernice had met and married a wealthy banker
and occasionally met up with Vivien for lunch in
London. Vivien thought love had cured her sister of
her extravagance. Lucca thought the banker had cured
it with his wealth.

Jock had become a jet-set dog with a fake diamond
collar. He had even featured in a spread in a fashionable magazine as a former rescue dog and he would
have become quite unbearable had he been able to
read. Lucca and he had become very fond of each
other but neither one of them would have admitted it.
Jock waited at the front door for Lucca every evening
and was rewarded with giant bones and chocolate
treats. Lucca said the rewards were training aids required to keep Jock from falling back into his old an-
tisocial habits. Basically all that meant was that Jock
only chased male visitors when Lucca was not around.

Three months after Pia's birth, Vivien was more
madly in love with Lucca than she had ever been. He
came up into the nursery while she was tucking Pia
into her cot. Their daughter regarded them with sleepy
brown eyes and yawned. Marco, whose days were
packed with relentless activity, was already fast asleep.

Lucca laughed softly. 'They're so quiet at this time
of day.'

'This place is magical,' Vivien contended, for she
revelled in the peace they always found at Il
Palazzetto.

Lucca let long fingers slide into her hair, his palm
curving to her delicate jawbone. His brilliant gaze met
hers with loving appreciation. 'You're the gold dust
in our lives, *amata mia*.'

Leaning into his tall, powerful frame, she let her soft lips open under the hungrily sensual onslaught of his mouth. She felt gloriously happy and loved. Home was inside the safe circle of his arms.

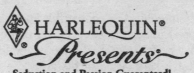

HARLEQUIN®
Presents
Seduction and Passion Guaranteed!

INTERNATIONAL DOCTORS

They're guaranteed to raise your pulse!

Meet the most eligible medical men in the world in a new series of stories by popular authors that will make your heart race!

Whether they're saving lives or dealing with desire, our doctors have bedside manners that send temperatures soaring....

Coming December 2004:

The Italian's Passionate Proposal
by Sarah Morgan

#2437

Also, don't miss more medical stories guaranteed to set pulses racing.

Promotional Presents features the **Mediterranean Doctors** Collection in May 2005.

Available wherever Harlequin books are sold.

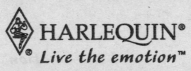

HARLEQUIN®
Live the emotion™

HPINTDOC

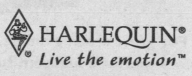

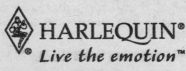